The door swung open. In it stood a woman nearly six feet tall. She wore a black turtleneck sweater and blue jeans stretched tight over her broad, firm hips. She looked tough. The tough look might have been her own. More likely it came from the .38 Smith & Wesson Airweight revolver that she pointed at my belt buckle.

I raised my hands slowly. I didn't take my eyes off the gun. You can always tell a serious shooter. They don't aim anywhere but at your belly.

"Son of a bitch," I muttered.

"What's the trouble here, soldier?" she drawled, in the soft, flat Montana accent that was born on the cattle ranches of Texas and carried north on the long drives. "By this point in the program you're supposed to have your clothes off."

Fawcett Gold Medal Books
by Fredrick D. Huebner:

THE BLACK ROSE

THE JOSHUA SEQUENCE

THE BLACK ROSE

Fredrick D. Huebner

FAWCETT GOLD MEDAL • NEW YORK

A Fawcett Gold Medal Book
Published by Ballantine Books
Copyright © 1987 by Fredrick Huebner

Library of Congress Catalog Card Number: 86-91828

ISBN 0-449-13225-0

Manufactured in the United States of America

First Edition: June 1987

For Christine

Prologue

He had to hit the man three times to kill him.

When the killing was done, he straightened and dropped the iron pipe in the dust. He was wet with sweat and shivered in the thin night-chilled air.

An older man stood beside him, his face half lit by the gas lantern he carried. The lantern was trimmed down low. The older man smiled.

"A hard thing the first time," he said. "But the power. The power you learn to like."

The younger man who had done the killing said nothing. He shook uncontrollably with the cold that seemed to come from inside him. When the older man reached out and caressed his cheek, he shook all the harder.

CHAPTER 1

I always thought that Bernie Seaton was the worst-looking soldier I ever saw. When I first knew him he had been a thin, shaky, serious-looking kid from suburban San Francisco. He was clumsy as a colt, the kind of dog soldier who couldn't keep the mud out of his M-16 or the fear out of his voice as he reported to a bored young second lieutenant at Than Son Nhut Airport. I remember that the airport asphalt had been sticky with Asian heat. As a jaded nineteen-year-old spec four with six months of South Vietnam behind me I had bet a beat-up lifer gunnery sergeant two packs of Camels that Seaton wouldn't last two weeks. Before the two weeks were up Bernie Seaton had saved my life and taught me that you never judge a person's worth by how he looks.

Fifteen years later Bernie Seaton looked pretty much the same. The wild, wiry hair had been styled into a short corporate cut, and the thick glasses had given way to contact lenses. But he still bent his thin frame into the same intense crouch over three thousand dollars of executive desk that he once had over a jeep tire, writing his

1

daily letter home. As he scribbled furiously on a legal pad he puffed nervously on a cigarette that he kept hidden in a half-closed desk drawer.

I knocked softly on his half-open office door. He straightened up with a jerk, slamming the desk drawer shut so hard that three volumes of the *Federal Reporter* fell over like dominoes on the top of his desk. He stood up, blinking in confusion, then he saw me standing in his doorway and smiled.

"Jesus, Matthew," he said, laughing shyly at his own clumsiness, "you really gave me a start." He walked over to me and shook my hand. "How are you, anyway?"

"Fine, Bernie," I replied. "You're looking good. But," I added, pointing to a gray wisp of smoke drifting from his drawer "your desk is gonna get lung cancer."

"Oh, for God's sake," he sighed. He opened up the desk drawer and put out his cigarette. "New policy in the office. I'm not supposed to smoke anymore. Coffee?"

"Sure."

As he sent out for coffee, I looked around. Bernie had a corner office near the top of the new Montana Pacific Building. It was shaped like a pentagon by the angled-glass outside walls of the building. The room was carpeted in beige wool. The rugs laid over the carpet were first-rate Persians. Walnut bookcases covered the inside walls. The desk was of matching walnut, bordered by a single strip of brass that ran around its top. I sat down on a cream-colored Italian leather sofa and looked out through the bronzed glass windows. Forty-five stories below me the 9:20 Bainbridge Island ferry emerged from a shroud of morning fog and docked at the foot of Madison Street. It was morning in America, just like Reagan says, and her corporate princes were living better than the Medicis ever dared.

Bernie sat down beside me. As coffee was poured, I

said, "You guys at Montana Pacific live very well, Bernie. If the guys back at the repair yards in Kalispell, Montana, ever saw this, they'd have some very pointed questions about why their wages were cut last year."

Bernie didn't laugh. Instead he looked pensive. There were new lines around his eyes. He was far too tired for this fine a morning. "This isn't my stuff, Matthew," he said stiffly, gesturing at his office. "The company owns it, and it can all disappear tomorrow."

"I know that, Bernie,' I said. "I'm sorry, I shouldn't try to be funny before lunch."

"No problem. Things are going pretty well for me. In fact, I'm in line to become general counsel to the entire corporation next year. If there's no trouble along the way."

"That's great, Bernie. But what kind of trouble?"

He poured himself some more coffee and leaned back wearily on the sofa, his hands laced together behind his head. Before he could speak, the telephone on the table in front of us began to ring. He let it ring once, then leaned forward and picked it up. He listened to the speaker, nodding. "We'll be in right away," he said. Then he turned back to me.

"A missing guy," he sighed, "by the name of Larry Kramer."

Randolph Whitten was in his late forties but looked younger, a tall lean man with a runner's build and something of an athlete's grace in his step. He had a long narrow face beneath lanky blond-gray hair. He wore a dark blue suit custom-tailored to show off his square shoulders and flat belly. He was trying to look like old money and older schools. It almost worked, except around the eyes. His eyes were the color of dirty gray ice.

"Rand Whitten," he said, shaking hands and ushering us to the conference table that stood to one side of his large office. "I'm the vice-president and chief of corporate operations."

"Matthew Riordan."

"I'm running a little early today," he said, glancing at a flat thin gold watch, "so I assume Bernie hasn't had time to fill you in completely, Mr. Riordan."

"We were just getting down to it, Rand," Seaton said.

"Fine. Let's start at the beginning. I assume, Mr. Riordan, that you're reasonably familiar with Montana Pacific's business.'

"It was hard to grow up in Montana and not know about the Montana Pacific Railroad," I replied. "The Montana Pacific and Anaconda Copper controlled the state for almost fifty years."

He let that pass. "Hmm. Well, Montana Pacific is much more than just a railroad today. Three years ago the corporation was restructured as a holding company, with the railroad as one of its subsidiaries. That was when the corporate offices were moved from Butte to Seattle. Today we're a diversified, multinational resources company, with transportation, mining, timber, and chemical interests." He talked like he was giving a report to the stockholders. "Two years ago, we began taking a serious look at the recreation market. Our first major project is the proposed White Rose Mountain ski area."

"I've heard of the project," I said. "It's in the North Cascades, out toward the Okanogan country, isn't it?"

"Yes, in the Manzanita Valley," he said with mild irritation—not a man used to being interrupted. "We've established a field office out there and completed most of the land acquisition, except for some Forest Service swaps for land held by the railroad. We don't expect too many problems there. At the moment we're doing our planning and design and preparing our environmental impact statements."

"There is some environmental opposition," Bernie cut in.

"There always is," Whitten replied testily. "At any rate, there's a problem with our environmental effort. Both Bernie and our regular outside counsel, the Wilkins, Hale firm, think it could be serious."

"What is it?"

"The head of our environmental survey team, a soils and water engineer by the name of Kramer, has disappeared. We don't know why."

"I'm beginning to see why you called me," I said dryly.

"What's that supposed to mean?" Whitten said sharply.

"It doesn't mean anything at all," I replied. "Much of my practice consists of referrals from law firms or corporations that may have a mess on their hands."

"We don't know that yet," Bernie said.

"No, but you need to find out. Soon."

"True enough," Whitten said, frowning. He rubbed his temples with the fingers of both hands, as if he had a headache, then stood up. He took off his suit jacket and tossed it casually on his marble conference table.

"Tell me a little about yourself, Riordan," he said as he strolled around his office. "You're here solely on Bernie's say-so."

"I'm an anachronism," I replied. "A lawyer in solo practice doing some criminal defense, internal corporate investigations, and whatever else comes in the door. I started out as a Justice Department investigator, and then a prosecutor. I also did three years in corporate litigation in New York City with Winthrop, Seward & Caldwell."

"They're a nationally recognized firm. Why'd you leave? Couldn't cut it?" There was an edge in Whitten's voice. I ignored it.

"In a way. They thought I was a good lawyer, but that I lacked an appreciation for the structured life."

"So you're a smart-ass," he said flatly.

"Correct."

Whitten strolled back to his chair and sat down. He fitted the tips of his long fingers together. The backs of his hands were dark with a health club electric tan, in contrast to the starched white cuffs of his shirt. He frowned again, silently.

I glanced at Bernie. He rolled his eyes. We waited. I looked around Whitten's office. It was polished wood and slick lacquer, its edges cold and harsh and sharp. I began to wish I didn't need the money.

Finally, Whitten said, "Tell me how you would approach this situation, Riordan."

"I don't have enough information to know yet," I answered. "The important thing is to find out if you have a problem. Right now there's maybe one chance in four that Kramer disappeared for reasons related to his job. That's what you have to focus on. I'd start out by taking a look at your field office, talk to people there, try to make a judgment why Kramer took off. If it looks like Kramer has a personal problem, you can leave it alone."

"No, we can't," Bernie interjected. "Kramer's written most of the EIS personally. We've been sued twice over the adequacy of the EIS, and there's a couple of other little land cases pending. Kramer's deposition has been noted three times. I can't put the court off for too much longer. I've got to have him."

"That's a tough one, Bernie," I said. "If he's taken off on his own, he could be anywhere. He'll be hard to find and harder to bring back, and even if you do, he may be a troublesome witness. Stall as best you can on your lawsuits while we try to figure out if there's a real problem."

"I think Riordan's right, Bernie," Whitten said. "But tell me, Riordan, how will you search for him? I don't want to have an army of private security types showing up in the Manzanita Valley. The environmentalists will find out, and they'll have a field day with us. The press will be terrible.''

''No sweat. If I need to bring in outside help, it'll be just one or two people, and they'll be both quiet and good. The real advantage, Mr. Whitten, in bringing in an outside lawyer to conduct an internal investigation is that most of what I learn and report to you will be protected by the attorney-client privilege. If the news is bad, you can release it to the public in a way that limits the damage to your company's reputation, and you'll get solid credit from the press and the government agencies for being willing to confront your problems and air them out.''

''Well, that all sounds nice and lawyerly, Riordan,'' Whitten said dryly, ''but I cannot stress the need for absolute discretion on this. Absolute.''

''I think you'd better define that, Mr. Whitten,'' I said slowly. ''Bernie's known me for fifteen years. He can tell you whether he thinks I can keep my mouth shut. But if you are asking me to bury whatever I find, forget it. I have a duty to you, but I have a larger duty to the courts that is part and parcel of my job. I won't be part of a cover-up.'' I stood up, very slowly, then shrugged into my suit coat. I didn't need the money that badly.

Bernie said, ''Matthew, wait. Nobody's asking you to cover anything up. This is ridiculous. It's premature.''

''I just want to know where things stand, Bernie. If I take your money I'll protect you to the best of my ability. But that's all I can do. It's also all you can do, Bernie. Anything else is cutting things too damn fine.''

''I think that's all we're asking,'' Bernie said.

There was a long silence. Then Whitten spoke. There was ice in his voice. ''I've never liked this damned project,'' he said. ''I don't like this mess. And I'm pretty damned sure I don't like you, Riordan.'' He hesitated, then added, ''But the chairman isn't giving me any choice. Bernie, set this up.''

CHAPTER 2

The firm of young, upwardly mobile lawyers that I used to sublet my Pioneer Square office from had grown ever upward, adding new young lawyers in devastatingly sincere blue suits until they had taken over the entire building and booted me out. After two or three months of increasingly desperate shopping around I had found another office. It was half of the upper story of a small office building, tucked amid the remaining salvage shops and ship repair yards on the north shore of Lake Union. It was miles from the courthouse, and such clients as I had didn't like the drive. But it had windows that opened to catch the water breeze and a narrow deck overlooking the lake, equally suited to breakfast or an after-work beer. And on summer mornings, birds sang.

The lower part of the building was taken up by a yacht broker with a nervous disposition and three ex-wives, no doubt complementary afflictions. I split the upper floor and shared the help of a secretary with an older lawyer in his fifties named Ken Stellman. He had once been a partner in a big downtown law firm but had been cut loose

8

in a reorganization. Now he serviced his few remaining clients by noon of each day and spent the afternoons waiting for the phone to ring, smiling sadly and shaking his head when I invited him out for tennis or a drink on a slow afternoon. It wasn't because he needed the money. He had been trained to work fifteen hours a day when he was still in his twenties. Now he couldn't stop, like an old fighter who fights again and again until beaten to the canvas by a younger man who always says it isn't personal.

On the way back to the office I had stopped to take out some fish chowder from the late Ivar Haglund's restaurant, a cedar-and-totem-pole palace for the tourist trade on Northlake Way. I sat down at my desk with the chowder and crackers and a glass of local chardonnay, the poor man's business lunch, and settled in to read the files Bernie had given me about Larry Kramer.

Larry Kramer was freshly forty, a time when a lot of men take a long hard look in the mirror and decide they're never going to be famous or rich or play wide receiver for the San Francisco Forty-Niners. His résumé said he had been born in Medford, Oregon, and had taken his bachelor's in geology and a master's in hydrological engineering at Cal. He had worked summers for the Forest Service since he was sixteen, then joined the Service full-time after graduating in 1971. As near as I could tell from his résumé, he hadn't done much forest ranger stuff since his early summers. He had been a technocrat, figuring out how logging or mining operations in the national forests would affect lakes and streams in adjacent areas. After ten years and a couple of promotions, he left the Forest Service to join Walters & Bertram, a Seattle environmental consulting service, doing the same thing for more money. He had joined Montana Pacific within the last year to work on the White Rose ski area project.

I could see why Bernie badly needed Kramer back. The

White Rose ski area would bring a hundred new problems to the remote Manzanita Valley. Cars and roads, lodges and shops, sewage and woodstove smog, hillside erosion and crime. There would even be, God forbid, condominiums.

Kramer knew how to handle big development projects, from designing them properly to prevent soil erosion and the destruction of fishing streams to calming down the locals fearful of making the Devil's bargain, trading their country peace for new jobs. The Montana Pacific had made him the chief author of their environmental impact statement, as well as their chief witness for project permit hearings before Washington State, Manzanita County, and the U.S. Forest Service. Without Kramer's testimony, much of the existing work would have to be redone. Construction of the ski area would be delayed for months, maybe even a year. With money at 12 percent, a delay like that would cost Montana Pacific a million dollars in interest payments alone. And probably cost Bernie his hard-won chance at the top.

I sighed and sifted through the rest of the paper in Bernie's file, looking for something that might give me a clue to the kind of man Larry Kramer might be. There wasn't much.

I found a picture of him in a suit standing with other staff members in a Walters & Bertram photograph from one of their ''This Is Our Team'' brochures. The picture was one of those phony promotional things, but I could see Kramer clearly. He wasn't a big man, but he looked wiry. He had a serious face, hidden behind a neatly trimmed brown beard and large horn-rimmed glasses, split by an uneasy smile.

The only other thing that said anything about Kramer the man was his insurance policy and tax forms. He listed as beneficiaries an ex-wife living in Everett and a niece in

Portland. He had no dependents named on his tax form or pension plan.

That was it.

Suddenly I wanted to find Kramer. Badly. Not because Bernie needed him, or even because I needed the money. I wanted to find him to get to know him, to flesh out the flat two-dimensional shadow man created from the scattered bits of file information and the fake cheerfulness of his company photo. As near as I could see, his life had been a series of okay jobs for not that much money, with no real chance of making a lasting contribution or a lasting change. He'd spent his time cranking out a few dry articles in dry technical journals and producing a pile of environmental testimony, facts and figures that only other bureaucrats would read, at last until somebody figured out a way to put in the fix. Then the pile of paper would be tossed away.

I wanted to talk to him and maybe learn from him, because I knew those feelings pretty well. And if I still had them at forty, maybe I would run away myself.

Bernie Seaton was supposed to meet me at the bar of the Alexis Hotel at six that evening to talk about Larry Kramer. At six-thirty he still hadn't shown up, so I settled in at the bar with a weak Chivas-and-water to wait. The Alexis is, at times, something of a yuppie singles bar, and at six forty-five I was deep in meaningful conversation with a lady banker of twenty-nine or so in a cast-iron gray skirted suit. She was very lovely and very smart, and she absolutely scared the hell out of me. If I'd stayed there another two hours we would have been speculating on the best private school for our firstborn. I was relieved when Bernie's secretary called and had me paged with a message to drop by Bernie's office. The only thing at the Alexis that night that was louder than the usual barroom noise was the sound of biological alarm clocks going off around the room.

The security guard at the Montana Pacific Building took me up to Bernie's tower office and dropped me off without a word. Bernie was sitting at his desk, stocking feet on the desk top, reading an open legal file that he held in one hand, holding a drink in the other.

"Bar's open," he said, gesturing at a bottle of Rémy Martin cognac on his desk.

"God, if it wasn't for the lawyers," I said, pouring myself a drink, "the distilleries would all go broke."

"Ain't that the truth," he replied. He sighed and tossed the file on his desk. He poured himself another shot. "The land acquisition for the ski area is just a bitch. You wouldn't believe the condition of land titles up there. Railroad grants, National Forest lands, homestead grants that have passed through three or four generations, mining claims—it's a mess. And somehow I've got to get us free and clear and settled out of lawsuits in ninety days. God."

"What happens if you don't?"

"The CEO doesn't have a ski area of his very own to take his grandchildren to. Whitten's always hated this project, and his departments would show a big loss for the year, so he'd be pissed. And everybody blames me. I'd probably get canned."

"I'm sorry. And yet I wonder if that would be so bad. You're killing yourself here.'

Bernie looked up at me, a little coldly. "I think that's my decision, Matthew," he said. "You made a decision not to reach for the top of our profession. Fine. But don't tell me what I should or shouldn't do. This isn't the war. And you're not my squad leader, trying to get me safely home."

I shook my head, embarrassed. "You're right. It's not any of my business. I'm sorry."

He smiled confidently. "Don't sweat it, Riordan. I'll work it all out yet. But I've got this cold nasty feeling that we've fucked up somewhere. Anyway, what'd you think of Larry Kramer?"

"If I was him, I'd run away too."

"Another cryptic Riordan comment. What's it mean?"

"It means I think he took off for his own reasons, and not because of problems on your project. Just look at his records, Bernie. The guy is middle-aging, divorced, nothing to keep him going but his job. A job is a lot, but sometimes it's not enough."

"And who does that sound like, Riordan?" he asked sarcastically.

"Sounds like you and me. That doesn't mean I'm wrong."

Bernie dropped his feet to the floor and sat up straight in his chair. "I know. Go on up to the ski area and see what you can find out. If it looks like he's skipped for personal reasons, figure out who you have to hire to trace him. I need him back. What's it going to cost me?"

"Ten grand retainer against both fee and expenses," I replied. "And don't look so pained. Whitten probably drops that much in French restaurants every month. On the company, of course."

Bernie laughed. "You're probably right. Okay, you've got it. How're you going to start?"

"Just like I said, I guess. But first I'll contact his ex-wife to see if she's heard from him. A lot of people have a weakness for their ex-wives."

"Not me," he said sourly.

"Oops. I forgot. Do not ask about Karen."

"Oh hell, it's all right," he growled. But he hesitated before he spoke. "She still lives over in Bellevue. That real estate guy she was dating moved in. The one with the

Porsche. She's happy, I guess. I was just too dull for her. Anyway," he said, "you still seeing Patty?"

"No, that was over some months back. We're friends, though."

There was silence for a while. Mutual self-pity is the worst form of social interaction. I changed the subject.

"How's the boy?"

"Oh, Peter's great." Bernie's face brightened. "A great kid. Just turned four. Smart as hell and, thank God, doesn't look a thing like me. He stays with me every weekend."

We fell silent again. I poured myself another drink and roamed around Bernie's office. The nice thing about being with an old friend is that you don't sweat the silences. I wandered aimlessly, listening to the small ticks and sighs that an empty building makes at night, looking at Bernie's pictures and the certificates that lawyers always hang to impress the client.

When I got to Bernie's Vietnam medals I stopped. They were mounted in a neat glass frame, surrounding the presidential citation. They were all there: the Silver Star, the unit citation, the Purple heart.

"It looks good, Bernie," I said finally. "Real good. I'm glad you put them up there."

"Karen had them framed when Vietnam vets became stylish," he said absently. "It fills a space on the wall."

"It does more than that."

"Not for me. Why should it? You know how I got those medals. I killed four other human beings. And do you know what's ironic? I barely remember doing it. You saw what I did. I got up out of that paddy and just started walking toward the VC machine-gun emplacement, shooting from the hip until I got close enough to take it out with two grenades. People have told me that. But all I remember of it is bits and pieces, like a broken film. I talked to a shrink about it, you know. He said it was called 'cognitive disassociation.' It's a kind of mental illness. It is not a distinction, in my book."

"You can call it what you want. There was, and is, a difference between the war and the soldier. Nobody gave you those medals for killing. They gave them to you for saving other people's lives. My life. For having the guts to do a morally repugnant thing."

"Maybe." He shook his head. "But I did learn something. When things around this snake pit are really bad, I just remind myself that I'll never have to do anything as rotten as Vietnam again. And for me that's enough." He stopped and poured himself the kicker drink for the evening, the one you need the night before but that gets you in the morning. Then in an old weary tired voice he added, "Just find my lost Kramer for me, Matthew. And if he's made a mess, try to get him out of it and keep him out of the papers if you can. Okay?"

"Okay," I answered.

CHAPTER 3

The Manzanita is a mountain valley in northern Washington State that runs from southeast to northwest, from the shore of Lake Chelan to the deep inner heart of the North Cascade Range. The valley floor has fine farms and orchards and ranches, sheltered by steep rock walls from the worst of the mountain weather. On the farms the second hay crop of the summer had been cut and rolled into giant bales to dry. Wildflowers grew in the grassy strips beside the highway. It was too early in September for the birches and alders along the Manzanita River to burst into yellow flame, but the day was summery and dry. As I rounded the southern shoreline of Lake Chelan, I felt strangely like singing.

Perhaps from relief. Early that morning I had interviewed Jennifer Woodard, Larry Kramer's ex-wife. She lived in Everett, the gently declining lumber city north of Seattle. I met her for breakfast at a diner near the elementary school where she worked. She was small and dark, a drawn, intense woman of thirty or so. She was clinically, even cruelly, indifferent to her ex-husband's problems.

No, she said, she had not seen Kramer in the year since their divorce, no weekends of latent romance or desperate second tries. There were no children and no support payments, just a split of their community property, on which Kramer still owed her four thousand dollars. Their parting had been calm and planned and final.

She knew that Kramer was working for Montana Pacific. She had never talked to him about his work, couldn't guess how he would react if he had gotten into trouble. He wasn't a drinker or a drugger or a chaser, particularly; one or two incidents, but that hadn't caused them to break up. Why had they? He bored her. She couldn't stand the thought of spending the rest of her life with him. Was there anything else she could tell me? No.

As I was going, she told me to remind him about the money.

Tolstoy said that all unhappy families were unhappy in their own way. He was wrong. Larry Kramer and Jennifer Woodard had divorced like so many other people had: anger and fear, remorse and pain, caring and resentment, and, finally, nothing at all.

Montana Pacific had located its offices in Darien, a valley town six miles down the road from the Cascade mountain meadow, halfway up Jack Pine Peak, that would be the site of the White Rose ski area. Darien itself was an insult to the beauty of the valley, a gritty little timber town that hung on to life by its broken fingernails. It was no more than five or six blocks wide, with low wood buildings scattered on both sides of the state highway. Darien ignored the Manzanita River as it danced between granite boulders at the edge of town. The town had been built fast and cheap, nothing more than a place to sleep while bleeding what wealth there was out of the nearby mountains. No one would mourn for it when it was gone.

For offices Montana Pacific had taken over the old Darien Hotel, three stories of ramshackle wood frame and peeling paint beside the rusting abandoned tracks of the Montana Pacific's North Cascades spur line. I parked the rented Chevy four-wheel-drive Blazer I was driving beside the hotel, grabbed my briefcase, and walked in.

The old lobby had been cleaned up some, painted white, and cut up into individual working spaces with beige fabric office dividers. As the door clattered shut behind me, a tall lean man with rimless glasses and long thinning brown hair poked his head over a divider. He looked like a puppet on a stage.

"Can I help you?" he asked.

"Maybe. I'm Matthew Riordan. I'm a lawyer working for the company."

"Oh, sure." He ambled out from behind the partition. He was dressed in a limp wool sweater and baggy corduroys. As he walked, the rubber cleats of his hiking boots squeaked on the wood floor. "I'm Doug Fedders. The Seattle office called and told us you were coming, but I didn't make the connection right away."

"It's okay," I said as we shook hands. "You were probably expecting somebody in a blue pin-striped rich man's suit."

"To tell you the truth, I was," he laughed, nervously. Then he stuck his hands in the back pockets of his pants and rocked awkwardly back and forth.

"I've never been involved with anybody who disappeared before," he began. "It takes some getting used to."

"Maybe you haven't yet," I told him. "Kramer's been gone only two weeks. That isn't much. Sometimes people just need to go away for a while, be by themselves."

"I hope you're right. Anyway," Fedders added, "what can we do for you?"

"I don't know yet. Suppose we take a chair and you tell me about your office here."

"There's coffee in the kitchen. Come on."

"Well," he said, after we were seated at a table in the old hotel kitchen, "there's only four of us, including Larry. He was the boss, in charge of the team. I'm the civil engineer, meaning I lay out the roads and the plan for the development. Andy McMichaels and Julie Keeler are both up at the site today. Andy does wildlife, Julie's a botanist, and they supervise the consultants in those areas who do species counts and stuff like that. We need that kind of detailed information for the EIS, the environmental impact statement."

"How did you four get along?"

"Pretty well. It's such a small office, nobody could or really would try to play politics."

"Did Kramer pal around with any of you in particular? Or date the woman?"

If Fedders resented the question, he didn't show it. "No on both counts," he said mildly. "Julie lives weekends with her steady, down in Wenatchee. It's pretty clear you don't know Larry, Mr. Riordan. He's a shy, remote guy outside of work. I think the most personal contact any one of us ever had with him was a Friday after-work beer."

"Do you know if he had friends, maybe a lady friend, here in the Darien area?"

Fedders shook his head. "No again, Mr. Riordan. We've only had this office open for six months, so I'd kind of doubt it. But I really don't know."

Fedders stood up and got the coffeepot, then filled both our cups. When he came back, I asked, "Bernie Seaton, the company's main lawyer, told me there was some fairly stiff environmental opposition to the ski area coming in. Has there been any friction with people in Darien, or in the valley?"

"Oh, not really." He leaned back in his chair, feet propped against the wooden table. "Most of the opposition comes from the big environmental groups in Seattle, Sierra Club and Friends of the Earth. They've filed the lawsuits, with one group of summer home people. I don't think they really expect to stop the project; they want to cut the best deal they can, minimize the impact on the national park, and our area sits just outside the border of the park. As for the people who live here year-round, they're mostly neutral or support the project. Logging and farming are both down, and times are pretty tough around here."

"So you haven't had any threats, anything like that?"

"Oh, no. Not at all."

I looked down at my notes. All my planned questions had been checked off, and I'd shot a blank. To Fedders I said, "Thanks for your time. When your other people come back, I'd like to talk to all of you. Right now I want to study the area maps and look through the files in the office here."

"Everything's in Larry's office. It's off to the side, so I guess it used to be the hotel clerk's old office."

"Kramer had a private office to himself?"

"Yeah, by popular demand. Larry has a pipe going from eight in the morning to the end of the day, nonstop. The rest of us couldn't stand the smoke. So we exiled him. Anything else?"

"I'm afraid I'm going to have to look through Mr. Kramer's personal stuff. Where does he live?"

"Right upstairs," Fedders replied. "He's fixed up an apartment on the top floor of the hotel, where the owners used to live. I'll get you an extra key whenever you're ready. I get off at five-thirty, so catch me anytime before then." He excused himself and went back to work.

I went to dig into Kramer's office. I had no idea what to

look for, but I thought I'd just use what I called Mickey's Razor.

When I was with the Justice Department I used to work with an accountant named Mickey Berenger, a slightly battered ex-merchant sailor with an accounting degree by correspondence and brains from God. Mickey had bad grammar and worse hygiene, and no big accounting firm would have hired him as a janitor, but he had an acute sense of smell when it came to going through a dirty set of company books. One thing Mickey was particularly good at was spotting the expenditures that didn't make sense until you turned them inside out. On one of my first cases he'd spotted a series of Holiday Inn charge slips that turned out to be a defense contractor's noontime chuckles with his personal secretary. The contractor had been a difficult, tiresome witness. After I showed those slips to his lawyer the contractor came into the grand jury room ready and willing to sing "The Bell Song" from *Lakmé* in any key I happened to like. And I learned Mickey's lesson: look for things that don't seem to make sense.

The company books for the White Rose project office made perfect sense. All big expenditures, including payroll, were handled out of Seattle. Kramer had controlled only a small office account that was meticulously posted in a neat, slanted engineer's hand. I could have checked the monthly totals with Montana Pacific's Seattle office, but it wasn't worth it. Kramer couldn't steal enough in Xerox fees and paper clips to help him run away.

Kramer's apartment on the top floor of the old hotel was kept in the same perfect order. There were four rooms: kitchen, bath, bedroom, and a study–sitting room. I tossed the first three quickly. Nothing hidden behind the flour, no cocaine in the bath salts, not even a girlie magazine tucked under the bed. There was a fair amount of clothing in the closet and the dresser drawers. Most of the bathroom stuff was there, but I didn't find a razor or comb; either he had no shaving kit bag or he'd taken it with him.

I slowed down when I got to the study. It was simply furnished: metal office desk, television, striped sofa, a promotional poster for the new ski area thumbtacked to one wall. I tackled the desk first. The desk was as ordered as his rooms, swept bare except for a desktop blotter edged in leather. His pipes stood straight up in the pipe rack on the edge of the desk. I picked up one of the pipes and looked at it. It was a fine Dunhill, a model that cost two or three hundred dollars. The expensive pipe surprised me a little. Kramer's taste in clothes and furnishings ran to K-mart or Sears.

I opened the desk drawers and began to go through each drawer, carefully. Kramer kept good financial records, neatly filed in the second and third drawers of his desk: charge slips, canceled checks, bills, bank accounts, stock statements. I went back to the kitchen and poured myself the last of the coffee and settled down to work.

The stock brokerage slips told me that Kramer had liquidated a couple of holdings in Boeing and in Schlumberger at a modest loss. The bank accounts—checking, savings, and money market—held balances of a couple of hundred dollars each. The charge cards had pretty hefty balances; on one card Kramer had paid the minimum for the past two months; two others showed that their lines of credit had been tapped for nearly two thousand dollars.

That didn't make sense.

Montana Pacific was paying Kramer the biggest money he'd ever seen, a salary of over forty thousand a year and bonuses. His living expenses in Darien were paid by the company, and he'd vacated the Seattle apartment he'd rented after his divorce. He was slow paying off his ex-wife. That wasn't strange, by itself—a lot of newly divorced men pay slowly, feeling the blow to their pride or something every time they write a check. But Kramer should have been swimming in cash. If you believed his books, he was almost broke.

Maybe he had taken off, for good.

I went back through the charge slips carefully, taking notes on where and when the charges had been incurred. It took me over an hour. As I finished, the sun was slanting through the west windows of the bedroom, soon to slide down behind the wall of the North Cascades and drop the valley into night.

I looked at my notes. There were gas charges in Wenatchee and Spokane, Washington, Coeur d'Alene and Kellogg, Idaho. One or two phone calls a week had gone to Whistler, Idaho. Restaurant and bar tabs from Whistler, Idaho. Charges every weekend at the Silver Bow Hotel in Whistler, Idaho.

What the hell was in Whistler, Idaho?

I went downstairs and let myself out and drove to the south end of Darien, stopping to check into a tourist cabin. Then I got on the road, south to I-90 and east to Idaho, aiming to find out.

CHAPTER 4

Whistler, Idaho, lies beside a narrow bend in the Selkirk River, in a valley tight as a billiard pocket, between the steep forested shoulders of the Coeur d'Alene Mountains. Whistler was the last of the roaring north Idaho silver towns that sprang up in the silver boom of the 1890s. Like the other panhandle boom towns, Kellogg and Wallace and Coeur d'Alene, it had been born almost full grown, with a turreted brick train station and a filigreed Victorian opera house amid the solid three-story brick commercial buildings in the center of town. The sheer valley walls surrounding the town had kept out the heavy smelters and fast food joints and trailer parks. The town had aged hard but well.

The Idaho panhandle is a remote, tight, tough place. It scorns the rest of Idaho, the Dale Carnegie boredom of Boise and the self-righteous conceits of the placid Mormon farming valleys to the south. The people are hard-rock miners, Welsh and Cornish and Slavic. The falling price of silver since the end of the 1970s had thrown a third of the miners in Whistler out of work, but they hung on through

24

the harsh winters, heating their eighty-year-old mill cottages with local wood and working half shifts at the few remaining deep-rock mines. They were waiting, I thought, for a time that would never come back, when the old storefronts on Cedar Street would have plywood taken off the windows and the pumps in the mines would clatter and whine and the men could go back to work again.

I parked my rented Chevy Blazer on Railroad Street, across the tracks from the rustling waters of the Selkirk, and stretched out to ease the road trembles in my legs. In the hills above the town a mine whistle blew. It was answered by the keening of fifty auto horns—the night shift's salute to a dead miner, probably killed the night before—that wailed for the two full minutes it took me to walk down Cedar Street and into the bar of the Cornwall Hotel.

The Cornwall Hotel had been built in the 1890s and rebuilt in the 1940s. In the bar, green-painted plasterboard and glass brick had covered over the original rough brick walls and high tin ceiling. Old promotional photographs from the Montana Pacific Ski trains of the 1950s hung on the walls. A map of the Montana Pacific's Coeur d'Alene branch line had been painted on one wall. Beneath the map an H.O. model toy train rested on tracks set on a narrow shelf that ran around the perimeter of the room.

I settled on a bar stool at the corner of the horseshoe-shaped Naugahyde bar. A sandy-haired bartender of maybe forty with a ragged nineteenth-century mustache drifted over.

"Drink?" he asked.

"Bourbon. A shooter and a draft," I replied. "Plus whatever you're having."

"It's after eight," he answered, pouring two shots, "and the boss is home for the night. Thanks." He brought the drinks over to me and we each put down the shot, then sipped at the beer.

"Just passing through?" he asked.

"Depends on what I find," I replied.

"Depends on what you're looking for," he commented. He was about to say something else when a voice rumbled from the far end of the bar. "Hey, Ted. Brandy neat and another Seven-and-Seven for Alice, okay?"

"Coming," he answered. I looked over at the far end of the bar. A white-haired old miner of maybe sixty-five sat with one arm wrapped around a smallish, sharp-featured, tightly permed woman of nearly the same age. The old miner grinned wolfishly at me. I smiled back.

The bartender named Ted returned. "Sorry," he explained. "Daniel's a good customer, but there's gonna be trouble when Alice's husband comes in later on."

I nearly dropped my beer on the bar. "Her husband?"

"Her fourth husband," the bartender said, smiling. "You stick around long enough, she'll probably give you a tumble." He sipped again at his beer and lit a cigarette. "So what brings you to Whistler? That's a friendly question. If you think it's not, let it pass."

"No problem. You want the straight answer or the line of bullshit?"

"The straight. Unless you're my ex-wife's lawyer. If you are, tell her she gets paid after the kids have new coats for the winter."

"I'm not. I am a lawyer, though. I'm looking for a guy who just checked out of work one day and never came back. He might have been through here."

"Maybe he doesn't want to come back. Sometimes people need a high hard lonesome."

"If that's the case I'm not going to drag him back. The people he works with need him, have got a lot riding on him. They want him back, no questions, and if he could just tell them that his problems aren't related to theirs, that might be enough. Here's his picture.''

As he began to study the picture I said something stupid. ''There's a witness fee for anybody who can lead me to him.''

The bartender set the picture down and gave me a stiff look. ''What's your name, friend?'' he asked softly.

''Matt Riordan,'' I replied.

''Let me tell you, Matt Riordan, that my name is Ted Keenan. And if you think I'll take your money to talk about somebody else's business, you can go straight to hell.'' He picked up what was left of his glass of beer and walked away.

I waited. Fifteen minutes later the bartender swept by and said, ''Bar's closed, man. To you. Six or seven others in town.''

''Give us two more beers,'' I said, trying again, ''and me two minutes to explain. Then I'll go.''

He looked me over again. ''All right,'' he said, and pulled down two drafts.

''I was wrong about you, but I'm not lying,'' I said. ''There's something wrong with the way this guy disappeared.'' I stopped, then added, ''We're not talking about a hard guy here. He's a quiet fellow who's gone through a bad divorce. He might be messed up, or into something he can't handle. I just want to find him. If he's okay, I'll leave him alone.''

Keenan chewed that one over, resting his bulky, ex-jock body on the back bar. ''Let me see the picture again,'' he said.

I handed it across the bar.

''Okay,'' he said finally. ''I've seen him. I think. He'd been coming in about once a week, maybe more, has a couple beers to wet the road down. Then he's gone for a while. Comes in later, plays some fairly serious blackjack, has a beer for the road, then takes off. But I haven't seen him lately.''

"Any particular day of the week?''

"Weekends. Maybe some weeknights, but if he was a weeknight regular, I'd remember him better.''

"Did he say anything that you recall?''

"No. The picture I get when I think of him is of a quiet little guy, wanting to fit in but somehow knowing that he wouldn't. Or couldn't. I don't think he ever won at blackjack.'' He shook his head. "Sorry, but that's all I get.''

"That's about right, actually. Thanks.''

"What makes you think he was coming into Whistler, anyway?''

"Oh, I found a lot of charge slips. From a rooming house, they say, but it seems awfully damned expensive for the panhandle. Eighty bucks a night.''

Keenan's face split into a broad weathered grin. "The Silver Bow Hotel?'' he asked.

"That's right,'' I said, surprised. "How'd you know?''

"Because in that hotel, friend, it's not just the room that comes expensive. It's the services.''

"No shit?''

"No shit. The Silver is one of three officially tolerated professional hook shops right here in Whistler, my friend. The last of their kind. One of the few businesses still making money in this goddamned town.''

"I'll be damned. I didn't think he was the type.''

"We're all the type, friend. When we're lonely enough. Just up to Zinc Street, then on your left. Tell 'em you know Ted.''

CHAPTER 5

The front door of the Silver Bow Hotel stood at the top of a flight of stairs leading up from a plain wooden street-level door in the heart of what had once been the banking street of Whistler. The front door was locked. I pushed the buzzer.

The door was opened by a short slender woman wearing a black leotard and a practiced smile. Her hair was bleached coarse blond. She would have been prettier had she left it dark to bring out the umber tones in her skin and the dark, almost Indian eyes, set in a face of high cheekbones and a wide, full mouth.

"Well, come on in," she said. "Welcome to the Silver. Can I get you a drink?"

"Bourbon on ice," I answered.

"Sure." She led me to a small sitting room with a red plush carpet and cheap paneled walls. I sat down on a sofa that sighed with the memory of a thousand anxious horny customers. I was still trying to find a spot between the broken springs when she came back with my drink.

"My name's Tracy," she said, handing me the glass. "What's yours?"

"Matt," I answered. Tracy was a name written down in Kramer's notebooks. It was just possible.

"So, Matt," she said brightly, "you looking for some good times or are you just shopping around on Zinc Street tonight?"

"Good times," I answered, putting a leer in my voice. "Think I'll do?"

"Why, sure."

"Then let's party," she said. She took my hand and led me down a long hallway to her room. The room was Spartan: a bed, a vanity and chair, a few cheap modeling posters thumbtacked to the wall. "Let's talk business first, baby," she said. "You tell me what kind of a party, I'll tell you the stake."

I took out a hundred-dollar bill and folded it lengthwise, once.

"What I really want to do is talk, Tracy. I'm looking for a guy I think you might know. His name is Larry Kramer. This is his picture." I handed a small portrait photo of Kramer to her. She glanced at it casually, then dropped it on the nightstand beside her bed. "All I want to do is ask you a few questions. I won't tell anybody what you've told me. There won't be any comeback on you."

"Uh, sure," she said hesitantly. "Whatever you want. But I've got to turn some money over to the house first. You wait right here." She took the bill and slipped out the door.

Like an idiot, I believed her.

Two minutes later the door swung open. Tracy was gone. In her place stood a woman nearly six feet tall. She wore a black turtleneck sweater and blue jeans stretched tight over her broad, firm hips. She looked tough. The tough look might have been her own. More likely it came from the .38 Smith & Wesson Airweight revolver that she pointed at my belt buckle.

I raised my hands slowly. I didn't take my eyes off the gun. You can always tell a serious shooter. They don't aim anywhere but your belly.

"Son of a bitch," I muttered.

"What's the trouble here, soldier?" she drawled, in a soft flat Montana accent that was born on the cattle ranches of Texas and carried north on the long drives. "By this point in the program you're supposed to have your clothes off."

"My daddy always told me I was a talker and not a doer.'

"You'd better do some talking now. Or you won't be doing any doing ever again."

"Sure thing, lady. My name is Matthew Riordan. I'm a lawyer, and I'm looking for a guy who used to work for one of my clients. His picture is right there on the night table."

She edged over to the night table and picked up the photo of Kramer I'd brought with me. Her eyes widened slightly in knowledge, then half closed as she put the picture down. She was good. The gun in her hand never wavered.

"You know him, don't you?" I said. "His name is Larry Kramer. Nobody wants to hurt him. All we want to know is whether he disappeared because of problems at the company he worked for."

"That's a nice line of talk, friend, but it's still a line."

"Lady, you can talk about me lying to you, but I am not the one holding the gun here. You are. And you have persuaded me to speak the truth. It's your call, but shooting me is going to bring down more trouble on you than you can fucking imagine. You are not in a business where trouble is something you can much stand. So put down the goddamn gun and maybe buy me a drink, because talk of my imminent demise always makes me thirsty, and I can level about what I'm doing with you and we can part friends."

She stared at me, gun leveled. My hand moved slowly toward a hardbound book on Tracy's makeup table. I had a little luck. It was a Ludlum novel, weighing three or four pounds. My hand edged closer. Throw left, roll right, hope for the best.

Finally the woman brought the gun up and laughed. "I really don't know why I believe you, Riordan, but I do. Come on."

She led me back down the narrow hallway, past three or four darkened rooms where an occasional chuckle or sigh could be heard through thin wooden doors, into a comfortably cluttered office. She sat down in a cushioned swivel chair and pointed to a straight-back chair across from her desk.

"Sit down, Mr. Riordan. What do you like to drink?"

"Nearly everything," I admitted, "but straight bourbon would be just fine."

She poured two drinks, adding ice and water to hers from a pitcher on her desk. I drank some of mine and said, "Thanks. I don't know your name."

"Laura Cantrell."

"I told you the truth about what I'm doing. I'm looking for Larry Kramer. He's been here, hasn't he?"

"Yes. He's been a regular for nearly four months now, on the weekends."

"Does he see any particular girl?" I asked.

"At first he moved around. Last two months or so it's just been one."

"Tracy, right?"

"Right. How'd you know?"

"The name was written in some of his stuff. Like a moonstruck kid."

"Oh, Christ, I should have seen it coming," she cursed. "What do you want? To talk to Tracy?"

"That might help."

"Why the hell should I let you? The customers here count on a certain amount of discretion."

"Because I'm not going to give you any choice. I talk to her now or I talk to her later. Later might mean cops and cameras and all sorts of things you won't like."

We looked at each other for a long time, each taking the measure of the other.

"All right," she sighed. "I'll get her in here." Laura Cantrell stepped into the hallway, then returned. "She'll be in here in a minute. Did this Kramer steal something from your company?"

"Nobody thinks so. He's important to getting a big project done, that's all. I want to talk to him, tell him that. If he took off for reasons unrelated to his work, I don't plan to drag him back to someplace he doesn't want to be."

She smiled. "That makes me feel a little better, I guess. I don't much like ratting on a man who's done nothing to hurt anybody."

"Nobody does." The door opened and Tracy walked into the room. She must have been going off shift. The leotard and stomach-tightening panty hose were gone. She wore a plain bra and panties under a fraying cotton robe. Her thighs were slightly pouched with fat, the skin of her belly loose. Her eyes were stripped of makeup and aged beyond her years.

"Tracy, Mr. Riordan here has questions for you. Tell him the truth," Laura Cantrell said.

Tracy merely nodded.

"Larry Kramer was a regular of yours, wasn't he?"

"Sure, almost every weekend."

"Why you?"

"I don't know. He liked me, I guess." She rolled her eyes with boredom.

"How much was he dropping on you a weekend?"

Tracy looked at Laura Cantrell with alarm. "Hey, if you think I've been holding out on the house, Laura, you're wrong. I—"

"Shut up and answer the man," Laura said.

"Two or three hundred. Sometimes he'd bring me presents, too."

"Like what?"

"Like clothes. Or . . . a little coke." She squirmed uncomfortably. "Laura, it was only when I'd be leaving the house the next day for my vacation. Honest."

"Tracy, you ever bring drugs in here again, you're through. No second chances, nothing." Laura Cantrell spoke grimly, her mouth tight.

Jesus, I said to myself.

"Well, what's wrong with that?" Tracy asked indignantly.

"Nothing, Tracy. Never mind. Did Kramer ever talk about going away, taking off for someplace and starting over?"

"No. I mean, sometimes he'd talk about wanting me to leave here and go away with him, but I always changed the subject."

"Did he ever say that he wanted to chuck his job, take off someplace?"

"No."

"Did he ever talk about anyplace he particularly enjoyed going to?"

"I don't think so."

"How about friends? Did he ever mention anyone?"

"No. I don't think he had many friends. He never talked about them." She yawned ostentatiously.

"When's the last time you saw him?"

"Maybe three weeks ago, maybe more. I can't remember. I wasn't exactly waiting up nights for him, you know."

"How did you feel about him? Personally, I mean."

"What a stupid question," she said, rolling her eyes again.

"Why is it stupid?"

"Well, for God's sake, he was just a trick. And he was old, too, nearly forty. He wasn't bad or anything, he was nice enough, but he wasn't nothing to me."

I didn't say anything for a minute.

Laura Cantrell said, "Anything else?"

"I can't think of anything."

"Okay, Tracy. Get some sleep. You're working tomorrow afternoon."

Tracy left, glowering at being questioned. I turned to Laura Cantrell. "Could I have another drink?"

"Sure," she said. She poured silently, then shrugged and poured one for herself. She lit a cigarette and said through the smoke, "You've had a little look at our business, Riordan. You don't look happy."

"I'm not. I'll bet he brought her coke or grass every time he came here. In all he was probably spending six, seven hundred a week on her. Kramer is a damned fool."

"At times all men are. Have you ever been with a whore?" She did not flinch at the word.

"Once. My sixteenth birthday, and my friends took me to the Miner's Wife in Butte. I suppose I was half drunk, but I don't remember it badly."

"No reason you should." Laura Cantrell sighed and added, "We've told you the truth here. What you can do is keep me out of it. Okay?" Her tone mixed threat and request.

"I will," I replied. "As much as I can."

"Well, I think you'd best be on your way. Unless you'd like the hospitality of the house. I suppose I owe you that after pulling a gun on you."

"Thanks, but I think I'll pass. Sex is sometimes like magic. It depends on blue smoke and mirrors. And I'm fresh out of illusions tonight."

She smiled and said, "We all are, Riordan." Then she led me back down the hallway to the door, and I walked down the steps back into the cold mountain night.

CHAPTER 6

It took the night operator at the Montana Pacific offices nearly ten minutes to track Bernie Seaton down. It was after ten at night, but when he came to the phone he still sounded wound-up and irritable, as if my phone call was taking him from work he was rushing to finish. As it turned out, it was.

"Well, what have you got?" he snapped. "I'm here in the law library, and it looks like all night isn't going to be enough time to figure a way around these lawsuits."

"You're not going to like it very much," I replied. "What little I've got tells me that there's something screwy with the way Kramer left. I don't think you should count on getting him back anytime soon."

"Shit," he said wearily. "Okay, start from the beginning. What did you find out?"

"I checked out Kramer as much as I could, talking to as few people as possible to keep the rumors down," I replied. "The guy's divorced, as you know, no family, not many friends. I've visited your office in Darien, talked to one of your people, checked out your books. If Kramer stole something from you or sold something about the company to somebody else, he did it well, because there's absolutely no evidence of a problem in your books or files.''

"So what's the problem?" Bernie asked. "That part sounds pretty good.''

"The bad news is coming, pal," I replied. "Kramer was broke, and he shouldn't have been. It turns out he developed some kind of fantasy thing for a whore over in Idaho. He's been seeing her every week for the past three or four months. And he wasn't getting any volume discounts, either. I'd guess she was costing him six, seven hundred a week, stringing him along.''

"So he needed money bad," Bernie mused, his voice fading a little over the long-distance line. "That makes him vulnerable to all sorts of temptations.''

"Yeah, but what?" I asked. "Everything at your office looks clean. There's one other thing that bothers me.''

"What's that?''

"The way he took off. His bank accounts are near empty but not closed. A little of his stuff is gone, but not all of it, and not the things you'd expect to be left behind when somebody disappears. His clothes are there, but his shaving kit isn't. He left his diaries. And his pipes. Good ones, two or three hundred bucks apiece. According to one of your people here, Kramer was a heavy pipe smoker, a real tobacco addict..You and I both know what that's like. Hell, for ten years, I'd have no sooner forgotten my cigarettes than cut off my hand.''

There was silence on the line. I didn't like delivering bad news. Bernie had troubles enough of his own, trying to bring the White Rose project off, and I sure as hell wasn't helping him. I began to wonder how much more stress he could take on before he cracked. But he was tough. The thing that made him tough was his belief that hard work and drive always paid off. I admired it but I didn't understand it. Not even Vietnam and law school had persuaded him that Horatio Alger was dead and Dick Diver was an asshole.

Finally, Bernie said, "I think you should take another pass at the office in Darien. If you don't turn up anything, come back to Seattle. Where are you now?"

"Truck stop. Just outside Post Falls, Idaho."

"Okay. I'll look for you sometime late tomorrow in Seattle, unless something turns up."

"Fine. Bernie, what's your problem with the lawsuits you keep talking about, anyway? Is it anything I can help you with?"

He chuckled. "This is the kind of law you hate, Riordan, remember? I'm tracking through and interpreting chains of title on some of the timberlands and railroad used to own in the Manzanita Valley. The ski area sits on a hodge-podge of federal, railroad, and private land. When those private lands were sold off for timber years ago, we sup-posedly retained the mineral rights. There's nothing on the land but gravel and crushed rock, but its good fill and building material. We used to open a pit every once in a while for roadbed repairs, stuff like that. Now we want to reopen some of the old pits in a big way, to provide for construction of the ski area, and the private landowners are screaming that we don't own the gravel. In some cases they might be right. I've already told Whitten that it could cost the company some money, and he sent me back down here to find some way to screw the landowners. Christ, the man's cheap. Probably how he got to be such a big deal in the company."

"I can help you with the research when I get back," I offered. "Just because its boring doesn't mean I don't remember how to do it."

Bernie said, "Thanks, pal, but its okay. We're screwed

on at least three parcels we've already taken gravel from; there isn't any reservation of mineral rights in the old deeds. And you can't build a title on adverse possession without something more than an occasional use. So we have to buy the land back, and now that the ski area is going in, the landowners will want a bundle. I've told the brass that; this is just to make me look good. I'll be done by morning anyway. But thanks.''

"See you tomorrow.'' I hung up the phone, bought a pint of medium-vile truck stop coffee, and got back on the interstate.

I didn't wake up the following morning until eight-thirty, still tired from the late night drive across the desert plateau on Highway 2, stiff from the buckboard ride of the rented four-wheel-drive truck I was driving. I grunted and groaned through a four-mile trot—only the charitable could call it run—down and back along the valley highway, then cursed the lukewarm water that was all I could coax from the tourist cabin shower. The Darien cafe scorched my bacon and vulcanized my eggs. It was my morning for complaining. Anybody who was cheerful to me without cause was going to find their smile knocked behind their ears.

I needn't have worried.

When I got to the Montana Pacific's office it was so quiet you could hear the dust settling. Doug Fedders stepped out from behind his cubicle with a grim look on his face. "Mr. Riordan? The Seattle office has been trying to reach you. I would have called you but I didn't know where you were staying."

"I'm sorry, I should have left the number last night. What's the problem?"

"Mr. Seaton. He was killed last night."

I closed my eyes. There was a high tight buzzing in my

chest. Bernie. He had survived so much. The war, school, divorce, a tough job. Too much. Not quite enough.

I must have stayed that way a long time. Fedders finally touched my arm. "Sir?" he said gently.

"I'm sorry," I said, coming out of my daze. "What happened?"

"He was killed in the parking garage of the MP Building. By a robber, they suppose. I don't know anything else. You're supposed to call Mr. Whitten."

"Thanks." I took the telephone number from Fedders into Larry Kramer's office and dialed. The number was Whitten's private line, and he answered it himself.

"Whitten, this is Matthew Riordan. I just got the news."

"Jesus Christ, Riordan, where have you been?"

"I was on the road last night, following a lead about Kramer. Got back here about four A.M. What about Bernie?"

"A terrible thing," he said with conventional insincerity. "Bernie was working late last night, left the offices sometime after midnight. Apparently some mugger attacked him in the garage with a tire iron. And killed him."

"Are the police there?"

"Yes. That is, they just left. A Lieutenant Ahlberg wants to speak to you. Our receptionist logged your call to Bernie last night. Ahlberg wants to know what you talked to him about. So do I."

"We talked about Larry Kramer. He's still missing, and the evidence he left behind doesn't really make any sense. Bernie was going to think it over and tell me what to do next."

"Come on in to Seattle, to the office. I'll want to talk to you before you talk to the police."

"All right, but let me call Ahlberg first. I'll tell him that I have to consult with you before I can tell him the contents of the telephone call. He's a smart cop, he'll understand that."

"Okay," Whitten said dubiously. "But tell him nothing about Kramer. Understood?"

"Fine," I said shortly, hanging up. I added "you son of a bitch" after the phone was safely dead.

I tried to block the memories of Bernie Seaton out of my mind as I drove back to Seattle, but the visions came away: Bernie piling sandbags in the Mekong Delta heat, sweat pouring from his skinny sunburned body as he worked to carry his share of the load; Bernie teaching Willis Page, a teenage soldier from deep in East Texas, to read, laughing with every triumph, then crying unconsolably when the boy was killed in an ambush. Bernie looking me up and taking me to dinner after I'd moved to Seattle, when I hadn't even thought to call him. Bernie, hurt and angry after his divorce, pouring himself into his job and his son.

Driving fast is a good way not to think. I flew down Highway 97 along the Columbia, breathing hard, watching the low autumn river swirl through the coulees above Rocky Reach Dam. Fifteen miles above Wenatchee I slowed a bit, watching for the State Patrol and letting the faster traffic pass me on the two-lane highway, trying to put my memories into a little box in the back of my mind, to be taken out another day.

A pickup flashed in the rearview mirror, coming up fast behind me. The pickup was pure drugstore cowboy, painted metallic blue and jacked up high on fat, oversized tires. The truck tailed me close for a moment, then flashed the high-intensity lights on the chrome rack over the cab. I wasn't in any mood to tolerate cowboy cutups, but I slowed and pulled over a little, driving with one tire on the concrete shoulder to let the damned fool pass.

The pickup swung left, straddling the centerline as it pulled up beside me. When it drew even to me I looked over at it, still mad, thinking to offer a choice word or gesture to the driver.

The words died in my mouth. The right window of the truck was open. A man with a round pie-tin face and longish brown hair swept back by the wind sat pointing a shotgun at my head.

I slammed the brakes and ducked as the gun let go, both barrels at five feet. The shotgun blast pounded the door and fender of my rented Blazer. I went into a braking skid as the rear wheels fishtailed out and the front wheels skittered sideways across the rough rock at the edge of the road. I fought out of the skid but ran out of open ground and sideswiped the Blazer into the roadside rockfall from the Columbia bluffs.

I shucked out of the seat harness and stuffed myself down at the floor for a long minute. I heard nothing but the wind that never stops blowing in the Columbia gorge, and the pounding of my own heart. Then I took a quick look through the driver's window.

The blue pickup was long gone.

The Douglas County sheriff's deputies who picked me up were polite and efficient. They had the Blazer, or what was left of it, towed to Wenatchee and drove me down to take my statement. There wasn't much I could tell them. I hadn't seen the license plate, and in that part of the state tricked-out pickup trucks are not just a hobby, they're a religion. When I declined to talk about just exactly what I was doing for Montana Pacific they grew mildly curious, but they agreed to wait for my statement to the Seattle police and sent me on my way.

The Hertz office in Wenatchee gave me a pound of accident forms, some curious looks, and a Ford sedan to replace the Blazer. I drove back to Seattle carefully, my right shoulder aching from bouncing off the dashboard of the Blazer. Aspirin didn't cut the ache. It was shortly after seven, almost dark, by the time I got back to Seattle. I parked the car in the basement garage of the Montana

Pacific Building and myself behind a double bourbon in the restaurant-bar on the first floor. Then I called Whitten.

He walked into the bar five minutes later, head back and shoulders squared. He paused to let his eyes adjust to the light, then stepped over to my table. He waved at a waitress as he sat down and ordered a designer mineral water. I ordered another double bourbon.

"I don't usually do company business in bars," he said stiffly.

"Ought to try it more often," I replied, finishing my first drink. "The chairs are more comfortable, and people would probably be a whole lot less scared of you."

"Is that some kind of snide comment about my management style?"

"Oh, Christ," I said wearily, "it's any damn thing you want it to be. Let's get down to business."

"Fine. What did you find out about Kramer?"

"He's missing, all right. But the way he did it doesn't look good." I told him what I'd told Bernie the night before.

"Great. Just great. The man we put in charge patronizes whores and takes off, leaving the company holding the bag. You aren't going to tell any of this to the police, are you?"

"I don't see how I can avoid it. I'm a fact witness now. The facts are material to a murder investigation and almost certainly relevant to an ongoing crime. The attorney-client privilege carries you only so far, Mr. Whitten. It normally doesn't justify obstructing the investigation of a capital crime, unless an individual corporate employee is claiming self-incrimination. That's my view, anyway."

"No one's claiming that there's a criminal conspiracy, Riordan. What happened to Kramer had nothing to do with Bernie's death."

"The hell it didn't. This afternoon two guys in a pickup

truck tried to take me out with a shotgun. I cracked my truck into a rockfall getting away. With any worse luck I'd be under forty feet of the Columbia River right now. I don't believe in coincidences, Mr. Whitten. Somebody doesn't want Larry Kramer found, and they killed Bernie Seaton. I think I should try to find out why."

"No!" he said angrily, slapping the table. "The company doesn't subsidize wild goose chases, damn it. Stay out of it."

"Don't you think," I said softly, fighting to keep my temper, "that you owe enough to Bernie Seaton to follow any lead relating to his death?"

"I'm sorry he's dead," Whitten said flatly. "We all are. His death is tragic. But he was just an employee, like anybody else. I've got to control this mess for the good of the company. The papers would have a field day with this. First Kramer, then Seaton. No. We'd get all kinds of bad press."

"This isn't a time for calculation," I said, still softly. "A friend, a good man, died. It's a time for doing the right thing. Even if the connection looked weak, it should be checked out. It can be done carefully, with discretion."

Whitten's face was set, his eyes hard. "This mess is all Seaton's fault, anyway. He hired Kramer. The way this project was going, I probably would have canned him anyway. As your client, I am telling you not to disclose anything about Larry Kramer to the police. If you want Bart Whipple to come down from our regular law firm to dress that order up in nice legal language, fine."

"Respectfully, I decline. I will protect your privileged statements and your best interests, have the police keep the information confidential, in accordance with my reading of the state code of ethics, but that is all I can do."

"You're fired."

I smiled. "You weren't listening," I replied. "I already

quit. You'll get my bill and a check for what's left of your retainer within ten days."

He stood up, staring, breathing hard. Then he caught himself and relaxed a little. "You dumb son of a bitch," he said. "You think you can push me around, don't you? You're wrong. We'll sue you for everything you've got. The word will get out. Nobody in this city will touch you."

"Go ahead," I said.

His eyes widened in disbelief. He turned and stalked away.

When he left I ordered another drink and got the telephone brought back to my table. I called the Seattle cops. The police switchboard managed to raise Vincent Ahlberg in his car, on his way home. They couldn't patch the call through, but they gave him the message and he said he would come back and meet me in fifteen minutes at the garage where Bernie had died. I tried to finish my drink, but it no longer tasted right, and I left most of it on the table when I paid the bill and walked away.

CHAPTER 7

One of the true tests of elegance must be how you look in a parking garage. Vincent Ahlberg passed. He was wearing a dark blue three-piece suit with fine chalk pinstripe, a J. Press shirt with the collar pinned down over a red silk tie, and black leather loafers that must have cost a third of a patrolman's take-home pay. After twelve on-duty hours there wasn't a wrinkle. Vince could have passed for a catalog model if he wasn't built like a concrete block. And wasn't standing in a parking garage next to Bernie Seaton's Honda sedan with yellow police crime-scene tape wound around the scene like ghastly ribbons.

I had met Vincent Ahlberg some years before, shortly after I moved from New York to Seattle. I had just opened my law office and was trying one of my first cases, a burglary defense for a snotty young punk whose father, a mechanic, paid my bill with a broken heart and his only real joy, a nearly restored 1971 MGB-GT coupe. The case was a loser from the start, but I hammered at the cops and the only eyewitnesses, shaking their testimony and nearly getting the kid off. When the jury came back in with a conviction, Ahlberg, who had been watching parts of the trial, caught me at the courtroom door and offered to buy me a drink. I was startled. I asked him why.

"Because," he said dryly, "some of you lawyers care more about your haircuts than you care about your clients. You tried damned hard. Call it a quirk. Let's go get that drink."

We did. Since that time we had been friends, cautiously but for real. When Bernie died, Vince, as head of the homicide squad, called the crimes-against-persons unit. And he was all business.

"Matthew," he said as he peeled off a leather glove and shook my hand, "you look lousy. Truly lousy."

"Suits my mood," I replied. "Tell me about it."

"Your friend Seaton was standing behind his car, trunk open, probably putting his briefcase away. Assailant came up behind him and hit him with a tire iron. At least four or five times. There's at least four entrances to this garage that are unlocked at night. Nobody saw a thing."

"It sounds like a bash and snatch," I said, with a coldness I didn't feel. "How's that play?"

"Not bloody well. There's a couple of pretty serious inconsistencies. The first blow knocked Seaton down and probably out; why keep hitting him? The wallet was taken, but one of my people found it in a garbage can on the next level. The cash was gone, but the credit cards were all still there. Seaton was wearing a stainless-steel Rolex; it was still on the body."

"He bought it years ago, in Singapore," I mused softly. "On R-and-R."

"What?"

"Nothing. Anything else?"

"The briefcase was rifled. Corners bent on file folders, papers wrinkled. Granted that a thief might look there, why go after the briefcase instead of the watch or the cards?"

"I don't know. It sounds like you aren't ready to write this off."

"Not yet. I want to hear what you have to say."

"Okay. But what I say tonight is just between you and me. Seaton's boss doesn't want me talking to you at all. Before I make a written statement I want to make sure I'm following the rules on revealing privileged information. It's a very close call, and I'd like to try and keep my license. Can you live with that?"

"I guess so."

"Bernie hired me to look into the disappearance of a man named Larry Kramer. Kramer was in charge of the early work on a Montana Pacific ski development out in the Manzanita Valley. Bernie was afraid he'd left because of some kind of trouble with the project. I was supposed to find him if I could, but mostly just try to figure out if there was a problem. The project looked clean, but Kramer's disappearance looked funny." I filled Vince in on the condition of Kramer's finances and his apartment, and tracing him to the cathouse in Whistler. "I talked to Bernie at ten to twelve or so, still at his office. He told me to check out a few more things, then come back to Seattle."

"Did Seaton sound unusual? Show stress, or say anything that didn't fit?"

"No. No more stress than he'd normally have, working against a deadline. He was working on settling out some mineral-rights claims, or something. I drove back to Darien. The next morning I got told he had been killed. I was driving back to Seattle when two guys in a pickup truck blasted me with a shotgun. I wrecked the truck I was driving but didn't get hurt."

"Get a look at them?"

"Yeah, but not much of one. I think I could identify one of them, but I'd hate to have to testify to it."

"You think these things are connected?"

"I don't know how. But the timing is too good."

"I suppose," he said sourly, "that it is. Thanks, Matthew. You've given me more questions than answers. As usual."

"Life's a bitch, and then you die."

"Yeah," he said, gesturing to a bloodstain on the concrete of the garage floor, "but not like that. Let's go."

Vince rode me home in his unmarked patrol car, gently suggesting that if I so much as turned the key in my rented Ford he'd bust me for drunk driving. As he dropped me at my house he told me to get some sleep and make my statement the next day.

I live on the northwest shore of Lake Washington, in a beach house I had inherited some years ago from my aunt, an artist and teacher who had built the house herself in the late 1940s. The city had grown up around the house since then, but my half-acre lot is still overgrown with alder and cedar, screening the house from the road on the hill above. I walked down the sloping path toward the house and stopped when it came into view. There were lights shining in the kitchen and living room.

Son of a bitch. Trying twice in the same day isn't fair. I stepped back into the trees and walked around the house. From the slope on the side of the house I jumped and caught the railing of the deck extending across the back of the house, above the walk-out basement. I swung a foot up and scrambled low over the railing, landing in a crouch beside the woodpile on the deck. I took a piece of alder from the pile as a club and looked through the French doors into my living room.

Patty Miller was sitting on the sofa, drinking wine from a stemmed glass. Reading Proust, a book club edition I could never finish, that she'd taken when she'd moved out six months before.

I laid the chunk of alder back on the woodpile, unlocked the French doors, and stepped into the living room. "Pats?" I said gently.

She dropped the book and spilled some of the wine. "Jesus, Riordan, you scared the hell out of me. What the hell are you doing sneaking in like that?" She tried to mop up with her hand the scattered drops of wine that had spilled on the coffee table.

"It's a long sad story. Buy me a drink and I'll tell you, if you like long sad stories."

"I write them every day. What do you want?"

"Bourbon, honey. Lots." She went into the kitchen to pour it.

Patty Miller was then a reporter for the Seattle *Post*. We had met a couple of years before, but had never really talked until last year, when she interviewed me for a feature on the dying breed of solo lawyers. The day she filed her story she let me take her to dinner, and I fell hard for her quick laugh and her go-to-hell ways and her long firm body that gleamed in firelight. A month after that she moved in; six months later she moved out, a case of two people who loved each other but couldn't live together without tearing each other up. After a month of silence I had called to buy her a drink and we started the long process of becoming friends. I had asked her out again. She refused, but she came by the house or office once a month or so, for a laugh or a meal or sometimes to stay the night. Sometimes we slept together on those nights, sometimes not, each of us more than a friend, a safe harbor of the heart.

She came out of the kitchen with my drink and kissed me gently. "I tried to call, but your office said you couldn't be reached until you got back today," she said. "So I let myself in and took a chance that you wouldn't be here with the queen of the senior prom. Or whoever. Sorry."

"It's okay," I answered. "I'm glad you're here. Really. What happened to that accountant you'd been seeing?"

"Christ, what a screaming bore," she said scornfully. "He was nice to look at, but he spends all his time adding up numbers and running marathons and talking too much about both those things. So I split."

"I'm sorry."

"Me, too. For a woman over thirty it's hard enough to find a Mr. Mediocre, much less Mr. Right. Can we talk about your troubles instead of mine? I'm already bummed out."

"Okay." I sipped at my drink and then got up and poked at the fire, not really anxious to tell the story again, not when I didn't know the middle, much less the ending.

"You know Bernie Seaton was killed last night," I began.

"Yes, I saw that in the paper this morning. Beaten in a parking garage. Christ. I know he was a friend of yours."

"I was working for him. A man named Kramer disappeared from the new ski area the Montana Pacific wants to build in the Manzanita Valley. Bernie needed him to testify in the lawsuits related to the project, and he was afraid that Kramer might have split because of some kind of scandal related to his work. I went out there. Kramer's gone, all right. I tracked him to Whistler, Idaho. He had the hots for a whore working in one of the houses there, but it was a dead end. When I got back to Darien, they told me Bernie had been killed. I started to drive back to Seattle when two apes in a pickup truck tried to take me out with a shotgun on the road. They missed, but not by much."

"Jesus." Patty took a long pull from her wineglass. "Are the two things connected?"

"I don't know. I think so. Bernie's boss at Montana Pacific doesn't; he wants a hush pulled over the whole thing. He fired me. You can't use any of this, by the way."

Patty put up a hand and stroked my cheek and said, "You're always off the record with me, kid."

"Sure," I said dubiously. "That's all I know. Ahlberg says that Bernie's killing doesn't look like a mugging, but he doesn't have much to go on."

"What are you going to do?"

"I don't know. Give it another couple of days. Maybe I'll call in Bernstein, have him see what he can do."

"Bernstein," she said archly. "You know, it took me three days to recover after his visit three months ago. And Kelly Walters, the woman I set him up with, is never going to forgive me."

"Eventually," I said evenly, "she will treasure the experience. What she can remember of it. That was Bernstein in party mode. When he's working, there isn't anyone better."

"I know you liked Bernie," Patty said, "but I don't see this as something you have to do. And you might get hurt. Let the police handle it."

"I can do things they can't. I don't have to be polite. And Bernie was my friend."

"Macho bullshit."

"No. Irish stubbornness."

"Same thing," she sighed. "Are you going to go back east of the mountains?"

"Probably. Why?"

"Because I need some help. With Keith. That's one of the reasons I came to see you."

Keith was her brother. I'd never met him; there was some sort of estrangement between them that Patty had never cared to discuss. All I knew about Keith was that he was about ten years younger than Patty and still lived in Colville Falls, in the far northeast corner of the state, where they had both grown up.

"What's wrong with him?" I asked.

"I don't know," she said, dropping her eyes. "He's had a hard time getting his life in order. He mostly just drifts. I haven't been able to reach him in nearly a month. I finally called a neighbor, and she said Keith hasn't been seen in weeks."

"That doesn't mean much. He's twenty-two and doesn't know what he wants to do in life. He may just be out on the road, looking things over."

"I know. Perhaps I'm just feeling guilty. Mother died when Keith was seventeen, still in high school. I was too wrapped up in my work to go back and take care of him, and I really didn't want him in Seattle. So I pretty much left him on his own. He managed, but I think he probably hates me for it."

I was about to put Patty off when I saw the evident pain in her eyes. "Okay, when I go over I'll drive up to Colville Falls and ask around. If he had charge cards or anything like that, Bernstein can run his charges through and see where he's been."

"Thanks." She dropped her head to my shoulder and burrowed down next to me in the cushions of my sofa, like a cat getting comfortable for a long winter nap. She told me about the arson story she was working on, her words coming more and more slowly until she dozed into a light sleep. After a little while I woke her gently.

"Time to sleep, kid," I said quietly. "You take the bedroom."

She opened her eyes and stretched and stood up, smiling at me, a smile I wished I could bottle and use on rainy Mondays. "I'm not going in there by myself," she said. "There are lions and tigers and bears."

I got up, a little stiffly, and took her hand. "We'll fight them off together," I said.

We did.

*   *   *

An hour later I still couldn't sleep, feeling that strange unease that sometimes comes in the middle of the night. I gently unwound myself from Patty's sleepy embrace and kissed her. She sighed and snuggled deeper into the covers. I got up and pulled on some sweat pants and padded out in the living room to make myself another drink. I made the drink and found an old Joni Mitchell album. I played it softly and listened to her sing of a lover with a madman's soul. Her voice was fluid and warm, and the song made me feel better. It was a song that I had played a lot when I was younger, and I remembered a time when I had been less of a cynic and Bernie had been less of a striver, a time that was as much dead unreachable history as the days of Imperial China.

I tried hard to close my mind off, and I padded quietly around the living room straightening books and magazines, looking for other small mindless chores to perform. Patty had said that there was a photo of Keith in her purse that I should take. I found her purse and the photo and stole one of her cigarettes and smoked it and looked at the picture. It was a high school graduation shot of a kid with a fringe of longish brown hair surrounding a round moon face. The picture had been airbrushed to take out his teenage acne, and most of the life had been taken out of the picture as well.

When it hit me that I had seen that face before, I called Bernstein and got him out of bed and told him to meet me in Spokane in the morning.

CHAPTER 8

I flew over the Cascades the next morning in a small de Haviland prop plane that skittered and jumped as it beat its way through the mountain headwinds and over the desert to Spokane. We landed just after dawn in a light rain that painted the airport tarmac silver. The plane was too small to use the usual jet plane gates, so it taxied to a parking area and we used the old-fashioned wheeled stairs to get out of the plane. I walked across the runway tarmac to the airport. I loved it. Whatever romance there is in flying died when people walked from their airplanes through long plastic tunnels that looked the same in St. Paul as in Seville.

I took a cab into downtown Spokane to the old Ridpath Hotel. Bernstein had promised to meet me there for breakfast, in the Lobby Grill, second booth on the right. Seven o'clock. I knew that Bernstein would be there. Bernstein is as Bernstein does.

What Bernstein mostly does is be the best, and maybe only, private detective in Kalispell, Montana. He is surely the only one with a Master of Arts in Foreign Policy from

Columbia University. I have known Bernstein since Vietnam, back when I was a grunt and he was in Army Intelligence, a name he regarded as inherently contradictory, if not downright impossible. After the war he became a full-time spook for the CIA. Sometime in the early Reagan years he had parted on less than amicable terms with the Company. He doesn't say much about it. Knowing Bernstein, that makes me wonder about the number of casualties. Now he lives on a ranch on the shore of Flathead Lake in Montana, reasoning, correctly, that it is the last place anybody would ever look for him.

Bernstein sat with his back to the wall, facing the entrance, his black eyes calmly taking notice of each person who walked through the door. He was dressed in working clothes: faded denim jeans, an old British army sweater in oiled wool with a shooting patch on the shoulder, lightweight hiking boots. The blue pin-striped bankers and lawyers having breakfast at nearby tables eyed him a little cautiously.

When he saw me come through the door he smiled and stood. We shook hands.

"Matthew," he said, in his quiet growl.

"You look good," I replied. "Thinner." Thinner on Bernstein is relative. He is about six feet high and four feet wide, as strong as an offensive tackle and a whole lot faster.

"Been working out more," he replied to my comment.

"Old age finally creeping up on you?" I kidded.

"Hell, no. We've got a new health club over in Kalispell. I'm dating the owner, so I get it free." He poured us coffee from a silver pot. "Food's on its way. Why don't you tell me what this is all about?"

"It's kind of complicated. A couple of things that probably have nothing to do with each other. Do you remember Bernie Seaton?"

"A kid in your platoon in Nam. Looks stupid but he isn't. How the hell is he, anyway?"

"He's dead."

"Shit. I'm sorry, I liked him."

"So did I." I told Bernstein what Bernie had been doing and why I had been working for him. He listened silently, sifting and organizing the facts as I spoke.

"So, what's the real problem with Kramer's disappearing?" he said.

"It looks wrong, that's all. The guy's bank accounts have been cleaned out, but all his personal stuff was still in his apartment. That's inconsistent. And as I was driving back to Seattle after Bernie's death, somebody tried to take me out with a shotgun on the highway."

"And you don't think that's a coincidence?"

"No. I sure as hell do not."

Breakfast arrived and we fell silent as a grimly efficient waitress served eggs scrambled with smoked salmon and home fried potatoes. When she left, I said, "I tried to talk to Bernie's boss. He thinks that Bernie's death has nothing to do with Kramer's leaving. At least that's the company line. When I disagreed, he fired me."

"So what do you want to do?"

"I want to find out who killed Bernie. The Seattle police are working on it, but Ahlberg's not hopeful. It was a professional job, I think. They hit him with a tire iron and tried to make it look like a mugging, but they went through his briefcase. A mugger wouldn't do that."

Bernstein was silent, thoughtful. Then he said, "I didn't know Seaton very well. Were the two of you close? How much do you owe him?"

"We weren't really close, I guess. I liked him and was working for him when he got killed. Once, a long time ago, he saved my life. I don't think I can just walk away. And there's a complication."

"What's that?"

"While I was home, Patty came to see me."

"That's a complication, all right. I thought you two broke up."

"We did, but we're friends. Or something. I told her about Bernie getting killed, and that I felt like I should keep working on it somehow. When I told her I'd be coming back over here, she asked me to do her a favor. Her brother took off from home about eight weeks ago. He lived north of here, in Colville Falls, where the two of them grew up. His name's Keith Miller. She doesn't know where he is, and she'd like to find him."

"I don't see a connection."

"Maybe there isn't. She gave me his picture. Remember I told you that two guys tried to take me out on the highway with a shotgun?"

"Get to the point."

"I saw the guy in the pickup tailing me, with the shotgun, just before he let go. And he looks just like Keith Miller."

After breakfast I gave Bernstein Larry Kramer's charge card numbers and he went off to call them in to his contact inside one of the Seattle banks. Fifteen minutes later he returned from the lobby telephone booth and sat down opposite me in the Grill. He picked up the front section of the Spokane *Chronicle*, glanced at the front page, snorted, and tossed it on the table. "If the world ended, that stupid rag wouldn't print it until three days later. And only after they cleared it with the Crowley family."

"So where do we stand?"

"Benny can run all three of the numbers you gave me back six weeks for any transactions. Cost you an ace apiece."

"Ouch," I replied.

"That look on your face leads me to a critical subject. How am I gonna get paid for this?"

"Patty and I will split your expenses. It'll break us, but I have our bankruptcy papers ready to go. Your time is another problem. I can't afford to pay you much, but I've got a bill in to Montana Pacific for what I've done so far. Patty said she'd offer you a weekend of illicit pleasure at Lake Quinault Lodge. I don't think I'm gonna let her."

"Bastard. Try and stop us. Okay, you're on the easy-credit plan. But if paying work comes up, I'm going to have to take it. I've got a payment due on the ranch in January."

"Fair enough. Let's go to Colville Falls."

CHAPTER 9

Colville Falls, Washington, is a study in shades of gray, an aging mill town near the Canadian border, nearly gone to hell. The cement dust from the Portland cement plant there blankets the town like a modern version of the plagues of Egypt. A few people in the town keep their battered 1930s vintage mill cottages painted in bright colors to ward off the dust, but most have just given the hell up, accepting the usual bargain. Dust in the air, dust in the lungs, dust you can see in the placid waters of the damned-up Pend Oreille River. Dust for jobs, for work, for pay, for self-respect.

Patty and her younger brother had grown up in one of those company houses, on Third Street, near the river. Bernstein parked his four-by-four pickup on the side of the unpaved street and looked the house over.

"Looks empty," he said.

"I've got a key."

We left the truck and walked up to the front door. The house was a rectangular box. There was a shallow porch, and windows on either side of the front door. Moss grew on the brown, asphalt-shingled roof. Dingy gray-yellow paint peeled from the clapboard siding.

Patty's key stuck in the lock, but I managed to work it loose and get the door open. We walked in carefully and quick-checked the five small rooms. Nobody home. We settled in to look the place over.

We started searching in the front parlor. The sour smell of old damp dust and half-burned green wood from the cheap woodstove assaulted us. The parlor had been furnished in the late 1930s and hadn't been changed since then. A battered Art Deco sofa in moth-eaten green wool stood along one wall. A couple of matching chairs filled the corners. Bernstein checked the furniture. He came up with a tattered paperback book and sixty-five cents in change. He kept the change.

"Making a profit already," he said.

The kitchen was a curtained-off alcove. Dishes were piled in the sink and on the sideboard. The refrigerator had stopped when the local public utility district had shut off the power. I opened it, then shut it quickly.

"New and unknown forms of life in there," I reported.

There were two small bedrooms. One contained a cheap fiberboard wardrobe and a double bed covered with a twisted pile of sheets and blankets. The other had been fitted out as a den. There was an old wooden office desk pushed against one wall. The other contained a fiberboard bookcase mostly filled with magazines and paperbacks. I searched the desk. Bernstein took the bookcase.

He whistled softly. "Not a nice boy, this Keith. Not a nice boy at all."

"What did you find?" I asked.

"Take a look. King James Bible. *Protocols of the Elders of Zion. Mein Kampf.* Army weapons manuals. A working collection of *Soldier of Fortune*. And this mimeographed stuff is from the National Socialist White Morons Party.''

"Hunh.'' I picked up one of the mimeographed tracts. In the center there was a two-page foldout. It showed the concentric circles of a rifle target. In the center was a black man, his back turned, running. I folded it up and put it back.

"Somehow I don't think the NAACP would approve,'' I said.

"Or B'nai B'rith. What was this little prick up to?''

"I don't know. I haven't seen anything that tells me where he's gone. Let's try the neighbors.''

"You don't have to, gentlemen,'' a querulous, old woman's voice said. "I'm right here.''

I turned around. An elderly woman, in her seventies at least, stood in the doorway. She wore a faded flowered house dress. Her hair was bound into tight gray curls. She cradled a 16-gauge shotgun in her arms.

"Don't mind the shotgun,'' she said. "I just didn't know who you were. I figured you weren't thieves, though. You had a key. And there ain't nothin' here worth stealing.''

"Did you see her? Or hear her?'' Bernstein demanded.

"No. And neither did you.''

"Goddamn it, I'm gonna have a long talk with myself about this.''

"Don't get riled,'' the old woman said. "Just 'cause I'm old doesn't mean I'm senile, or can't still walk nice. If you'd like to talk, come over to my place, next door. I've water on for tea. And besides,'' she said, wrinkling her nose, "my house don't smell like a dead cat. Come on.'' She turned and walked out of the house.

I looked at Bernstein. He shrugged. We followed.

The old woman's name was Elizabeth Whitely. She lived next door in a house that was the same as the Miller house on the outside. Inside it had been paneled and papered and crammed full of old but solid Victorian furniture. Bernstein and I sat in the front room as Mrs. Whitely poured tea. After she poured the tea she came around with a bottle of Canadian whiskey and added a healthy slug to each cup, winking as she poured. Then she settled into a padded rocker covered in chintz.

Bernstein took slug of whiskey and tea from his cup, smiled, reached for his cigarettes, then quickly put them away. "Oh, that's all right, young man," Mrs. Whitely said. "Ernest"—she pointed to a framed sepia photograph on the wall—"used to smoke a pipe, so I'm quite used to tobacco."

Bernstein lit his cigarette and blew smoke gratefully out of the corners of his mouth.

"Now," she said, "what brings you here?"

"My name is Matthew Riordan. I'm a friend of Patty Miller," I answered. "This is Mr. Bernstein. She asked us to look for her younger brother, Keith. He's been missing, and she's worried."

"Took off about six weeks ago, Keith did," she replied. "But how is Patty?"

"Fine. Very successful. She's a senior reporter for one of the Seattle papers."

"Always knew she'd do well. Keith's another story. Ten years younger than Patty. He should have gotten out of this dying town, like she did, but he was missing something in here, I guess." She tapped her fragile chest. "Anyway, as I said, Keith took off. Didn't tell me where, of course. I'm just the nosy old neighbor."

"We found a lot of hate books and magazines in Keith's room, Mrs. Whitely," I said. "Mostly against blacks and Jews. Why would Keith have that sort of garbage around?"

"I don't know," she sighed. "He was laid off about year ago, at the plant. Since then it seems like he's been in and out. When he's in town, he has two or three mean-looking friends around with him, raising hell at the tavern and such. I don't know why he'd hate blacks or Jews, we don't even have any around here. Except Mr. Rosenberg, who runs the grocery store. And he's as nice a man as you'd ever hope for. I hope that doesn't sound patronizing, Mr. Bernstein. I take it you're Jewish too."

"I am and it doesn't, ma'am. Could I have another cup of tea?"

"Surely." She handed him the whiskey, then the teapot.

Bernstein poured. "Thank you. What were the men he was hanging around with like?" Bernstein asked.

"Worthless. One of them looked like an ex-con. Pasty. They probably had something to do with that damn church. Excuse the French."

"What church?"

"Oh, the White Nations Church of God, or whatever. It's over in Idaho, between Priest River and Sandpoint. You know. It's those crazy near-Nazi people, the ones in the news all the time."

"Is there anyone else in town we might talk to who might know where to find Keith?"

She frowned, thinking. "I doubt it, Mr. Riordan. Keith's not had much to do with anybody in town since his mother died five years ago. But . . ." She hesitated. "I hate to tell you, because she's a nice girl, but Keith's old high school girlfriend might know something. The two of them went out for years. Gretchen. Gretchen Meeker, but I just spoke to her mother at the store yesterday, and she said Gretchen married another fellow. Bonner was his name, I think. They live over in Sandpoint."

I stood up to go. "Thank you, ma'am," I said. "We'll try to find Keith and get him together with his sister. But if he comes back, just ask him to call Patty. Don't mention us."

She sighed. "Trouble?" She asked.

"It could be."

"I see. Well, I'm happy to help."

Bernstein stopped at the door as we were leaving. He took the old woman's hand. "Thank you for the best tea I've had since my grandmother was alive."

Mrs. Whitely smiled. "What did she put in it, Mr. Bernstein?"

"Polish vodka."

The old woman laughed and said, "I'll have to try that. Good day."

Gretchen Meeker Bonner lived on Lake Street in Sandpoint, Idaho. Sandpoint lies on the shore of Lake Pend Oreille, in the far northern part of the Idaho panhandle. It's a pretty tourist and timber town, the latest in a long line of western towns like Aspen and Santa Fe where California's rich and wellborn buy second homes and pretend they're just folks. On any given summer day in downtown Sandpoint the Mercedes sedans with California plates mix uneasily with the battered Japanese pickups driven by the locals.

The Bonner house was a small but lovingly restored turn-of-the-century Craftsman bungalow. The house was well back from the street, behind a quarter acre of trim green lawn and fifty-year-old maple trees just beginning to turn red with the fall. Bernstein and I were careful to stay on the sidewalk as we walked to the front door from the street.

A young woman answered the door on the second ring. She was pretty in an old-fashioned, Currier and Ives sort of way, with a sweet round face and long straight hair gathered back into a French braid. She wore baggy blue jeans and a loose shirt, as though she were pregnant and just beginning to show.

"Yes," she said patiently as she answered the door.

"Mrs. Bonner?" I asked. She nodded. "My name is Matthew Riordan. My friend and I are looking for Keith Miller. We thought you might be able to help us."

She didn't answer. A look of confusion and something like fear passed over her face. At that moment a pickup truck pulled up on the street behind Bernstein's truck. A brawny red-haired kid of twenty-five smiled and waved as he stepped out of his truck.

Gretchen Bonner yelled, "David!" as she slammed the front door shut in our faces. The smile fell off David Bonner's face like a stone. He reached inside the cab of his truck and came up with a kid's baseball bat, and brandished it like a club as he charged up the front walk.

I had just started to say, "Relax, pal," when Bonner took a swipe at me with the bat. I jumped back, stumbling on the edge of the grass. Bernstein didn't wait. He stepped inside Bonner's next looping wide swing, blocked the bat, got the other hand fastened on the arm with the bat, stepped, turned, and dumped David Bonner like a hundred-pound sack of meal dead on the ground.

The fall knocked the wind out of Bonner and he lay still. Bernstein casually picked up the bat from the ground and prodded Bonner beneath the chin, gently. "You okay, kid?" he asked.

Bonner's mouth worked as he fought for breath, then he finally managed to creak out, ". . . Okay. My shoulder."

"It's going to be a little sore," Bernstein agreed. "I did my best not to dislocate it. But you didn't give me very much time."

Together Bernstein and I got Bonner to a sitting position, then to his feet. As we did his wife burst from the house.

"David!" she cried. "Are you okay? I'm so sorry, honey. I just didn't know who they were." She got both arms around him and hung on tight. He smiled and gently worked her loose, tucking her in under one of his arms, her head barely reaching his shoulder. They fit well together. I smiled.

"We're sorry as hell to scare you, Gretchen. But we don't mean any harm." To David Bonner I added, "My name's Riordan. This is Bernstein. We're looking for a guy named Keith Miller. We were told your wife used to know him. We were about to ask her about him when you pulled up."

He shook his head ruefully and grinned, his teeth white against his red beard. "Sorry I swung. But you mentioned Miller's name, that's why Gretchen was scared. The son of a bitch just won't leave her alone. Anyway," he added, "I could use a beer. You guys want one?"

"Sure do."

"C'mon, honey," David said to Gretchen. "I'll help you get it."

The Bonners led us through their house to a glassed-in back porch. The sun had broken through the clouds and warmed the porch. Bernstein and I sat in a couple of rattan chairs, sipping cold bottled beer and listening to Gretchen's story.

"Keith and I both grew up in Colville Falls," she began, "and we knew each other all through school. In high school we dated, but I didn't see much of him after that. He went to work at the cement plant, and I moved down to Spokane. I took some commercial art courses and got a job in an advertising agency. Two years ago I moved back to Colville Falls to take care of my mother when she got sick, and I started going out with Keith again. He was only working half shifts by then, and pretty soon he was laid off. I tried to talk him into moving away, at least as far as Spokane, but he wouldn't go. Just drank and hung out with his friends. Finally, last year, I broke it off and moved back to Spokane when my mom got better. Keith kept coming around to see me. It was really embarrassing. I mean, not too long after that I met David, and we'd come back from a date and there would be Keith, waiting outside my apartment. God." She shook her head. "So childish. But his friends were worse. Some of them were really tough. And they started coming around with him."

"When did that start?"

"About six months ago. Just before David and I got married and moved to Sandpoint. I thought our moving away would solve the problem. But Keith kept coming around, even after I was married. He'd started going to some church near here, a crazy one."

"The White Nations Church of God?"

"That's it. Once I saw Keith in this uniform that they wear in church. He looked like a Nazi."

"When's the last time Keith came around?"

"About two months ago. I told him for the hundredth time to go away, that I was married, that I was pregnant. He didn't listen. Sometimes I don't think he cares, or cared, about me. He was never that . . . physical. He just didn't want to lose me, because that would hurt his ego or something. Anyway, David came in about then and threw him out. Keith took a swing at David, and David beat him up pretty bad."

"It was stupid," David Bonner broke in. "I should never have hit him. He and his idiot friends have been back, though. First they just kind of watched the house. Then they threw a rock through the living room window about six weeks ago. There was a note on it. The note just said, 'This could have been a bomb.' " Anger darkened his face. "What makes these people so damned mean, anyway?"

"Stupidity," Bernstein said briefly.

"What will you do now, Mr. Riordan?" David Bonner asked.

"I guess we're going to church," I replied. "I've read a little about this group. They have a Wednesday-night service, don't they?"

Bonner nodded. "I think so," he said.

As Bernstein and I left, we stopped at the door to thank Gretchen and David for their time and their beer. Gretchen smiled, but her eyes turned serious and she said, "If you see Keith, please ask him just to stay away."

Bernstein smiled at her with his very best happy snarl.

"We'll be sure to tell him," he said.

CHAPTER 10

The White Nations Church of God had its own compound, built on a hill overlooking the Pend Oreille River between Sandpoint and Priest River, Idaho. Bernstein and I had to double back three times on Highway 2 until we spotted the faded, four-foot-square wooden sign that marked the muddy gravel road that led to the church. Unlike every other church I'd ever run across, this one didn't seem to believe in advertising.

We turned off the highway and slithered up the muddy road in four-wheel drive. A quarter mile from the highway a metal gate topped with barbed wire blocked the road. A brown-stained guardhouse, hammered together from warped plywood and scavenged two-by-fours, stood next to the gate. The guardhouse had a chapel roof and a short flagpole topped with a cross. An American flag flew from the pole. With a swastika where the stars were supposed to be.

We stopped. A kid of perhaps nineteen stepped out from the guardhouse. He wore a baggy gray twill uniform with flag and swastika patches and a gray forage cap. He would have looked like an underage bus driver except that bus drivers seldom carry around an AR-15 Armalite, the semi-automatic civilian version of the military M-16.

He pointed the rifle at me as he walked around Bernstein's truck to the driver's side. I was driving. I rolled down the window.

"What you want?" he demanded, slurring the words. Pale blond hair drooped from under the forage cap. His eyes were weak blue and watery. His face was acne-scarred. His overbite would have had an orthodontist dreaming of tax shelters.

"We're looking for a friend of ours," I said pleasantly. "Fellow named Keith Miller. We heard he was a member of your church, and thought somebody here might know where he was."

"Could be I do, could be I don't." Country cagey.

"So let us in and we'll talk about it. Keith's been gone for a while and his sister's worried about him."

"Hunh." He looked at Bernstein. "Who's that?"

"Friend of mine. Friend of Keith's sister, too."

"Hunh," he said again. "Your friend looks like a goddamn kike to me. So he ain't gonna be no friend of Keith's."

"Just let us talk to the pastor. There's a service tonight, isn't there?"

"At seven. But your kike friend has no business here. Neither do you. Get lost."

"Hey, kid, be reasonable. All—"

"Get out!" he shouted. He raised the rifle and pushed it in my face. "Now, you Jew-lover. Now."

I looked at Bernstein out of the corner of my eye. He sat very still, eyes watching the moronic guard. His right hand dangled below the edge of the seat. There was a hideout gun taped there. A long tense moment passed. "Okay," I said finally, my voice quiet. "I'm gonna back up. Don't shoot."

I shifted the truck into reverse and backed it slowly down the muddy track. A hundred yards back down the road there was a wide spot, and I backed into it to turn around. The slight curve in the road left us out of the line of sight from the gate. I stopped the truck and dropped my hands from the wheel. My hands shook slightly.

I looked at Bernstein again. He faced straight ahead.

"What do we do now?" I asked.

He didn't say anything. He reached underneath the seat of his truck and came up with the hideout gun, a .45-caliber automatic. He checked the action, locked the safety on, and slipped it in the pocket of his down vest. When he looked at me his eyes were absolutely opaque. "Wait until dark," he replied. "And Matthew—"

"Yes?"

"There's a .38 automatic locked in a box behind the seat. When we find a place to stop, I'll get it out for you."

"I'm not sure I want it."

"I figured that. But it's my way or no way at all, because I don't like these people worth a damn."

We found the remains of an old logging road across the highway that led to a clearing in the brushy forest. From the clearing we could look down to the place where the church's road joined the highway. We waited. The sky darkened as clouds moved in and loosed a cold steady rain.

The White Nations Church didn't have a wealthy congregation. Most of the cars I spotted turning into the church's drive for Wednesday-night services were either rusty four-by-four pickup trucks or elderly Chevies and Buicks driven by equally elderly couples. The trail of cars petered out toward seven o'clock, proving that the kid at the gate hadn't lied about the time of the services. At ten after seven we pulled on hiking boots and gaiters to handle the muddy ground and started out, cutting across the dense, tangled, second-growth forest toward the church compound.

We were less than a mile away, but it took us nearly half an hour, going across rough wet overgrown country, to get to the barbed-wire perimeter fence surrounding the compound. I hoped the church services ran long.

As a fortress the place wasn't much. The church and its outbuildings were constructed of plywood and concrete blocks, painted white. At the far side of the square formed by the buildings stood a prefab log house. There was a guard tower beside it. The yard between the buildings was lit up by floodlights.

Bernstein cut through the fence with heavy wirecutters, then turned back to me. "Their lighting's lousy," he said. "If we stay to the right, we can come up on the church from behind. They won't be able to see us."

I followed Bernstein as we circled, crouching, staying close to the fence. When the church steeple blocked our view of the guardhouse, we cut across the overgrown field and sprinted up to the church, flattening ourselves against the side of the building.

An electronic organ inside the church pounded out the heavy strains of a German hymn. When the music stopped, I stuck my head over the base of the window and looked inside. The congregation was praying. Their heads were bowed. Their arms were raised in a stiff-arm salute.

"Jesus," I whispered.

"Let's take it around the corner," Bernstein said. "I think there's a door."

"Can they see that side of the building?" I hissed.

"Fuck it. These people are idiots. Amateurs," he whispered back.

"Don't you wish, you kike," drawled a voice behind us. The voice was high and almost choked with laughing excitement. "Get your hands up."

We raised our hands and turned around, slowly. The teenage guard from the gate who had stopped us earlier stepped forward, his rifle held waist high but still pointed at us. "Hey, Scott," he crowed. "I got two intruders."

A second man stepped out from behind the corner of the church building. He was tall and sandy-haired. He wore the same baggy gray uniform under a down vest. He held a long-barreled revolver in one hand, and pointed it carefully at us.

"Take their guns, Lee," he said. The boy stepped forward and shoved us against the side of the church to search us. He took our pieces and gave them to the second man. Then he bound our hands with throwaway plastic cuffs. "I'll be damned," the tall man drawled in a soft Texas accent. "Take 'em inside. The Reverend will want to talk to 'em for sure."

The kid took up his rifle and pointed it at us as the sandy-haired man led the way. Bernstein shook his head and muttered.

"Shit," was all he said.

The office of the "Reverend" Robert Anders Birdsall was done up in somebody's Sears Roebuck notion of what a great leader's office should look like. A thick carpet was laid on the board floor. A secondhand oak office desk had been refinished into somber dark brown and mismatched with a tan leather chair. The walls were knotty pine. A swastika flag hung on one wall. On another there were matching framed portraits. Hitler. And Christ.

When Birdsall walked into the room his goons stood to attention. He smiled and waved them at ease. Birdsall was in his fifties, a short man with wavy iron-gray hair and a politician's smile. He was dressed in a brown military suit with a white scarf draped over his neck. He reached into a small refrigerator and pulled out a bottle of beer, twisting the cap off with gnarled veined hands. He set the bottle on his desk, then carefully lifted the white silk scarf with embroidered crosses from his shoulders. He folded it carefully and put it away in his desk.

"Well, what have we got here, Lee?" he said to the boy. He took a pipe from a rack on his desk, filled it with Cap'n Black tobacco, and began tapping it with a finger.

The boy still had excitement in his voice. "These're the two I stopped at the gate today, sir," he said. "Caught them sneaking around behind the church during service. They had these." He dumped our automatics on Birdsall's desk.

"Say now," Birdsall said, "these boys look serious. Thank you, Lee," he added, "you can take the tower now. Must keep a watch out."

"That's all right, Reverend," the sandy-haired man called Scott cut in. "Lee's done good work. He should get the night off. I'll take the tower." There was an odd note of tension in his voice.

"Now, Scott," Birdsall replied patiently, "Lee must do his duty. Right, Lee?"

"Yessir," the boy said, and left.

"He's still a boy, Scott," Birdsall said when Lee had gone. "And boys talk too much."

"You're right, sir," Scott replied. He motioned us to sit down on a tweed sofa opposite Birdsall's desk. He remained standing, across the room, revolver drawn.

"Excuse me a moment," Birdsall said, lighting his pipe. He drew smoke and blew it out with a sigh. "I do like a beer and pipe after preaching," he said. "Even a man of the cloth is entitled to a few vices."

"Funny color cloth," Bernstein said, motioning with his cuffed hands toward Birdsall's shirt and leather Sam Browne belt. "Brown."

Birdsall laughed. "I suppose you think that's an insult, don't you? It's not. I am not a Nazi, Mr.—what is your name.?''

"Bernstein."

"Figures. I am not a Nazi because I am not a socialist. I admire Adolf Hitler as a great moral teacher, one who understood the plague of Jews on the white race, and found the right answer, total separation of Aryan whites and Jews."

"Murder," Bernstein spat. "Murder as policy. Murder as an industry."

"That's a lie!" Birdsall exploded, screeching. "Those 'death camps' are a Zionist plot! Stocked by Jewish criminals with German war dead. A vile, vile lie!"

"You are blind," Bernstein said. "And stupid."

A harsh red flush rose in Birdsall's face. He sputtered with anger, then suddenly stopped, calming himself. His eyes gleamed with mad serenity.

"We don't hate you, Jew," Birdsall said. "We whites want to be free from your Zionist control of the schools, the banks, the government, even"—he dropped his voice to a conspirator's whisper—"the telephone company."

I rolled my eyes. I was muddy, cold, tired, sore, and listening to a raving lunatic who had his own toy soldier pointing a foot-long gun in my face. Why? This made even patent law look good.

"Excuse me, Mr. Birdsall," I cut in. "We only came here to look for Keith Miller. We were told he belonged to your church. We tried to come in properly, through the main gate, but your guard wouldn't admit us. We mean you and your group no harm."

"Speak for yourself," Bernstein muttered.

"Shut up," I said to Bernstein quietly. To Birdsall I added, "Keith's sister asked us to look for him. He's been missing, and she's worried."

"I see," Birdsall said. He looked almost kindly, all the

anger washed away. An emotional chameleon. "She should not worry. Keith has been a member of my church, but I understand that he's gone off to California to find work. I spoke to him before he left, and he assured me that he would attend a Christian Identity church down in Glendale. He's a fine young man. He will call when he has established himself."

"Thank you," I said with complete insincerity. Legal training has its uses. "With your permission, we'll leave."

"Certainly," Birdsall said grandly. "We harm no one who does not harm us."

The man named Scott abruptly broke his silence. "Reverend," he said urgently, "I don't like this. I've seen guys like this before. The big Jew is too smart. He came through the fence in just the right place. He could be FBI, or worse, a spy or killer for the kikes in Israel itself. Let me have them for a while. I'll sweat them. Find out who they really are."

"It's not time yet, Mr. Griggs," Birdsall replied softly. "Our brethren in The Order did not know that, and they were destroyed. We are not yet ready, not yet strong. I don't doubt the truth of what you say. But for now, we shall send these two back to their masters in the Conspiracy as a way of showing our contempt." He spoke ponderously, like the Old Testament, King James Version.

"All right," Griggs said dubiously. He stepped over and untied our hands. Again he seemed oddly nervous. I began to wonder why.

"I will return your weapons," Birdsall said. "Their claws pulled, of course." He backed the rounds out of the chamber on each of our automatics and pulled their clips, dropping them in a desk drawer. Birdsall held out the empty guns like an offering.

I took them and put mine away.

"One last thing, Jew," he said to Bernstein. "You are

in the bastion of the Aryan race here. That is not permitted. If you return, I cannot guarantee your safety.''

Bernstein took his gun from me and put it in his pocket. ''When I come back here, old man, you'll die,'' he said evenly. Griggs slapped Bernstein across the back of the head with the butt of his gun. It was like hitting a rock. Bernstein never made a sound. He held Birdsall's mad eyes with his own.

''Think about it,'' Bernstein said.

We left.

CHAPTER 11

Bernstein and I jogged down the muddy road away from the White Nations Church, our breath making plumes of fog in the cold gray night. Bernstein said nothing. He was not a happy man.

"At the risk of having you take my head off," I said as we reached the main highway, "I think we should find Keith Miller and see if we can pull him out of this mess before you come back here and burn these bastards out of their hooches."

"I don't know why," Bernstein replied. "He's garbage, just like the rest of them."

When we reached his truck, Bernstein opened the cab and dropped the tailgate. We sat on the lowered tailgate and pulled off our muddy hiking boots and gaiters.

"I've never seen you like this," I said. "You've always been the most perfectly controlled, rational man I've known. But ever since we met that boy Nazi at the front gate you've been treating this like your private holy war."

Bernstein said nothing. He peeled off a muddy nylon gaiter and looked at it in the light from the pickup, then shrugged and tossed it into the bed of the truck. He pulled a half pint of Jim Beam from the pocket of his down vest, took a deep swallow, and passed the bottle to me.

"Last year I went to Tel Aviv," he began. "On business, but I had some free time and went to the Museum of the Holocaust. I'm not religious, but now I understand the psychology of religious experiences a little better. Because I had something like one." He took the bourbon back from me and took another swallow.

"I realized that I am a Jew. It's not the most important thing in my life, but it's where I start from and where I finish. I can't ignore it. You should go to that place, Matthew. See what the Nazis did. The crime is so enormous that people can't really comprehend it. Even the Nazis themselves couldn't deal with it. They turned the murder of six million people into just another government make-work program, with the usual blank-faced bureaucrats and unintelligible procedure manuals. To Americans now, it's a sad but slightly shopworn piece of history. The people who talk about it, like Elie Wiesel, are treated with the same kind of polite condescension usually reserved for missionaries, or people in the Peace Corps."

He shook his head. "And here—in my own damned backyard—I find a bunch of stupid clerks dressing up in Nazi uniforms, chanting all the old words like they want to conjure up all the old evil." He took one more hit from the bottle. "You know what bothers me most? The absurdity of it all. You heard that old man. I'm his enemy *because* I'm a Jew. It's like killing somebody because they're a shoe salesman. It's insane." He grimaced. Then he added, "But it's not something that can be forgiven. Hitler started with a small group. Remember the Munich Beer Hall *Putsch*, in the early twenties? It could have been stopped then, easily." He paused. Then he said, "This time things will be different. If I have to burn every last one of those bastards myself.''

I let Bernstein's softly spoken threat hang on the air. A rising moon brightened the sky, but the air was still, broken only by the hum of passing cars on the highway below. Finally I said, ''Keith Miller is twenty-two years old. He's broke, and he's at the least stupid to fall into something like this, but I promised his sister I'd try to find him. I think that means still alive. I need your help, but it's got to be on those terms.''

Bernstein's eyes were black and his face was like stone. ''I'll let you know if any of those charge numbers for Larry Kramer turns up active,'' he said. ''Let's get going. I've got lots to do. And a long drive home.''

I caught the last flight out of Coeur d'Alene to Seattle at twelve-thirty, getting back to Seattle a little after three in the morning. It was too late for the bars and too early to go to work, so I drove home through the quiet city, hoping to get a few hours' sleep before Bernie Seaton's funeral later that morning.

It didn't work. I fought the sheets for a couple of hours, too exhausted to sleep, then gave up and got up. I went down to the office at eight o'clock, as alert as a failed suicide but not nearly as cheerful. Patty was calling on the telephone as soon as I walked through the door.

''Matthew?'' she said anxiously. ''What did you find out?''

''Nothing that's going to make you very happy,'' I replied. I could see her in my mind's eye as I spoke. Her desk would be scattered with notes and clippings, the display terminal of her computer would be glowing green, her nails would tap anxiously on the desk top. ''Keith took off about five weeks ago,'' I said. ''None of the neighbors know where he is, and your old house looks abandoned.

He joined a white neo-Nazi church in northern Idaho some-time in the past few months. Bernstein and I went there. Things got a little rough. The preacher, if you can call him that, is a head-case named Robert Birdsall. He says that Keith moved to California.''

"Do you believe him?"

"No."

"Damn," she sighed. "What do we do now?"

"I don't know, Pats. Your brother's of age. If he wants to put swastikas on a bus driver's uniform and think he's rough, you can't stop him. You're a little late to start trying to bring him up now."

"Why are you trying to make me feel guilty, Mat-thew?" she asked in a cold, tight voice. "I do that fine all by myself." She slammed the phone down.

I sat at my desk and sighed and remembered that the size of my mouth was one of the major reasons Patty and I no longer lived together. I waited a minute or two, then called her back.

"I didn't mean that the way it sounded," I said when she picked up the phone. "I'm a little short on sleep this morning, as well as brains."

"I'm sorry," she replied. "It's just that I get—"

"I know, Pats," I cut in. "I think we've had this conver-sation before." Several hundred times, I added mentally.

She sighed again. "Is Keith in trouble?"

"I don't know for sure. He's been doing screwy things, mean things, hanging out with a couple of ex-cons, harass-ing his old girlfriend, joining that damned church. And there's one thing I didn't tell you the other night. I got a look at the guy who took a potshot at me on the highway the day Bernie died. He looked just like Keith."

"Oh, God." Her voice was very small and very soft. "Why would Keith do that?"

"I don't know, but I'll keep thinking. In the meantime, can you do something for me?"

"Sure. I think I owe you a favor."

"Bernie's funeral is at ten. I'd like you to go with me. I think I'm going to want a shoulder to cry on."

They buried Bernie Seaton a little after ten-thirty that morning. The cemetery was on the north side of the city, near the university. It had a lovely view over part of the campus and Portage Bay. A lot of Seattle cemeteries are like that, built on hilltops that overlook the city. I don't understand why. Certainly the customers don't care about the view.

It was a good funeral, as such things go. The scattered remnants of Bernie's family were there: ex-wife, son, sister, a mother clearly in shock from the unnatural death of child before parent. A few downtown lawyers, some of them Bernie's casual friends, had shown up. A small contingent from Montana Pacific stood off to one side, as if members of a delegation from a foreign government. Randolph Whitten stood in front of them, lean and tailored and correctly somber. We didn't speak. It was just as well. He looked at his watch three times during the brief graveside service. If he looked at it one more time I was going to break every bone in his body.

A light mist fell and silvered the rolling green lawns. A Presbyterian minister said some nicely nondenominational things about Bernie's prospects in the next frame. Patty and I queued up to place a final hand on the coffin, Pats hugging me for support as we waited. We said some nicely polite things to Bernie's ex-wife and young son. Bernie's son, Peter, clutched his mother's hand and looked bewildered. He would understand such things soon enough.

When the funeral was over, the sun filtered through a break in the clouds, giving us a sun-shower. I almost felt better until I turned away from the grave and saw Lieutenant Vincent Ahlberg standing behind me like a sentinel, a reminder of grim reality.

Vince wore a black raincoat, a stripeless black suit, a white shirt, and a black tie. His black shoes gleamed. He wore black dress gloves. He could have starred in a Hitchcock movie just the way he was.

He took off his gloves to shake hands, first with Patty, then with me. After the usual greetings, I said, "I'm surprised to see you here, Vince. It's a nice touch, but you don't really expect to find the killer here, driven by remorse?"

"Stranger things have happened," he replied. He took a small cigar from a leather case and lit it, cupping his hand to shield his match. "Actually," he continued softly, "when I became head of the crimes-against-persons unit five years ago I made it a practice that the investigating officer attend the funeral. Sometimes the families appreciate it. And it reminds us that in almost every case the victim was a normal person who left behind people who care."

"There are times—not often—when I regret having called you guys pigs fifteen years ago," I told him.

"There are times," he answered with a twisted smile, "when I sit down with some of the old boys and we remember laying the batons on your heads. We miss it. We liked it." He paused, smiling, then added, "Where the hell have you been, anyway? You were supposed to come down for a statement yesterday."

"Something came up," I said blandly, glancing at Patty. Her eyes were worried. "I had to leave town for the day. I'll come down now if you want."

"Might as well. I'm going to have a word with the ex-widow. Or whatever the hell you call them." He moved off through the thinning crowd easily, like a blade.

Pats waited beside me in pensive silence as Ahlberg

walked away. "Are you going to tell him what you suspect about Keith?" she demanded.

"I'm going to have to tell him sooner or later. It might as well be now."

"Why? You don't know for sure that it was Keith who shot at you. His involvement with these right-wing nuts has nothing to do with Bernie's death."

"Don't ask me to start believing in coincidences, Pat. I'm too old and too mean for that. These things connect somehow."

"Heaven forbid I should ask you to believe in anything," she answered angrily. "Anything but your own self-sufficient life. This is a twenty-two-year-old kid, Riordan. Show some heart, for Christ's sake."

"Bernie Seaton was beaten to death at thirty-seven," I shot back. "He left a four-year-old son behind him who'll need some answers someday. For all I know your kid brother killed him. Show some heart."

"Go to hell," Patty hissed. She stormed angrily across a quiet green meadow to the gravel parking area. I watched her get into her treasured, if somewhat elderly, Porsche 911. She cranked the engine over, kicked the Porsche into gear, and threw gravel ten feet as she spun away.

I kept watching long after Patty left. When Vince Ahlberg returned, he looked at me sharply.

"Something wrong?" he asked.

"It's funny," I replied, "how two people really have to love each other to really know how to hurt each other."

"Hilarious," he growled. "After your second divorce you'll learn how to laugh. Let's go."

CHAPTER 12

I made my statement in Vince Ahlberg's office, on the sixth floor of the Public Safety Building, popularly known as the Cop Shop. The Public Safety Building was built in the steel-and-glass style of the early 1960s, but inside it seemed much older. Three shifts of cops worked there each day, twenty-four constant hours of sweat, smoke, and fear. It was good that steel and concrete were stronger than cartilage and bone. If the building had possessed human frailty it would have collapsed long ago.

I made the statement as complete as I could, walking the fine line between obstructing justice and buying into a lawsuit from Montana Pacific. When I finished I was sweating. I walked out of Ahlberg's glassed-in office and got a Coke from the machine in the hallway. When I came back, Vince had sent the police stenographer away and was musing over a fresh cigar. "I think you can tell Patty to relax, Matthew," he said. "I just don't see any logical connection between her brother and his crazy church and Bernie Seaton's death. And I'm not sure your identification of Keith Miller as the shooter means that much to me.

I'd never admit to it in court, but eyewitness testimony under stress really isn't very good." He shrugged. "I could be wrong. Some crazy things have come out of the north Idaho mountains. That neo-Nazi group that was convicted of racketeering last year—The Order—they were involved in everything from bank robbery in California to the killing of that talk-show host in Denver."

"It doesn't make a whole lot of sense to me, either," I told him. "But it's a connection, and I'm going to push it for a little while longer."

"Then what?"

"I don't know. Go back to the office and draft some wills, maybe try a car crash case or two. The rent has to be paid, whether or not I can find Larry Kramer or Keith Miller or figure out who killed Bernie Seaton."

"Do that. This is one windmill you don't have to tilt at. We'll find Seaton's killer."

"Don't bullshit me, Vince," I said coldly. "I think you're trying to be a nice guy and make me feel better, but don't bullshit me, because it's not going to work. You've got nothing on Seaton's killer, nothing at all. And unless you start looking at the outside chances, you're going to stay with nothing until the papers have lost interest and the thing can be buried. Damn it, I've gone out on a limb to tell you everything I can. It's going to get me sued. Don't write this thing off yet."

"I'm not writing anything off," he said angrily. "I'm telling you that if you get back on your horse like the Lone Fucking Ranger, somebody out there might just try and knock you off again. And next time it might work."

When Vince finished yelling, the two of us were standing on opposite sides of his desk, leaning on our fists, our faces a foot apart. Vince's face was red. Mine probably was too. I choked back a snotty reply and said, "Why are we arguing?"

Vince sighed and sat back down at his desk. "I don't know. I should never argue with a lawyer; you guys think it's fun. Okay, I'm stuck with you poking around on this thing, at least until your money runs out. Is there anything else we can check out for you? We just love to be of service."

"There is," I agreed quickly, ignoring the sarcasm. "I'd like to know more about one of the people at the White Nations Church. This guy seemed to know Keith Miller, or at least about him. He looks like an ex-con to me. I'd like to see his record, if he's got one."

"What's his name?"

"Griggs. Scott Griggs."

Ahlberg led me to a small computer room to the side of the squad room. A uniformed patrolman sat at one of three IBM PC units, checking a list of addresses against some kind of index. The patrolman was young and black. His nameplate said "GAYTON."

"Morning, Mike," Ahlberg said to the patrolman. "Can I get you to run a name on NCIC?" NCIC is the National Crime Information Center data base.

"So long as I'm trying to make detective," Mike Gayton replied, "you can get help on the computer anytime.' He broke out of the program he was using and switched to NCIC.

Ahlberg grinned. "I like this man's attitude."

"When he makes detective he's going to call you Honky," I said.

"I do that now," Gayton said serenely. "Give me a name, if you've got one."

"Scott Griggs."

In a few seconds, Mike said, "I've got two of them. First one is currently in Raiford prison, in Florida. He's black. Second one is male Cauc', thirty-nine years old.

Scott Alan Griggs. Came out of Deer Lodge prison seven months ago.''

"Sounds good," I said. "Let's check the physical description.''

"We can do better than that, man," Mike said. He tapped a key and the computer color monitor screen filled with a rough facsimile of the bony angled face of Scott Griggs.

"That's him," I said. "He was at the White Nations Church when Bernstein and I got caught sneaking in, trying to talk to that crazed preacher, Birdsall. I'll bet Keith's neighbors up in Colville Falls would recognize Griggs, too."

The patrolman tapped another key. "Picture will be here in about ten minutes," he said. "Anything else?"

"Let's take a look at his record," I answered.

The screen filled with a list of dates and events. "Too good to waste this," Gayton said. "I think we should print it out." He tapped the print key, and a printer began to stutter.

I studied the screen as the printer worked. Griggs had an honorable discharge from the Army, but that was about the last good thing he'd done. There were California convictions for theft and assault, a New Mexico bust for car theft, and the last, long conviction was for armed robbery of a gas station in Miles City, Montana. While in Deer Lodge prison he had been a member of a white-supremacy gang and had been disciplined for provoking a brawl with Hispanic prisoners.

"Nice guy," I said as I finished reading the screen. "Ivy League man."

"Terrific," Ahlberg agreed. "Want to see what he's doing now? We've got parole reports."

The screen refilled with new information. Griggs had had a job waiting for him in Bellevue, Washington, when he got out. At last report he was still working there, as a security guard for the American Freedom Foundation, a right-wing fund-raising group. Wilbur Hayes, the president of the foundation, had requested the special parole dispensation. The out-of-state parole had been approved quickly. Montana had been only too happy to see Griggs go.

"I think he and I need to talk," I said.

Somehow I stumbled through the rest of the day at the office, clearing out the mail and using soft words and soothing tones on a couple of irate clients who'd been trying to reach me for three or four days. By five o'clock I was convinced that there was a little man operating on my skull with a chain saw and a rusty pick. He was doing a pretty good job until Grace Dwyer, my elderly, but not motherly, part-time secretary returned from the store down the road with a bottle of aspirin and a six-pack of Heilman's Special Export Beer.

She held them up. "This is my act of Christian mercy for the year," she said. "Do yourself a favor. Go home, get a little sloshed, go to sleep."

"A sovereign remedy," I agreed. "Thanks, Grace, I'll do that."

"Good night."

After a while I opened a beer and took it out on the porch with me. The sky had cleared since Bernie's funeral that morning. Now it was streaked with red and orange and indigo. The lights of the downtown office buildings were coming on, and they reflected brightly in the calm water of Lake Union.

I had nearly drifted into sleep when the phone rang. The answering machine was on and I almost said to hell with it, but I hauled myself out of my deck chair and over to the phone before my twenty-second spiel was over. I punched the tape cutoff button and said hello.

A woman with a warm, deep voice and a soft Montana

drawl said, "Matthew Riordan? Did I wake you up? I thought this was your office telephone."

"It is, but I can sleep anywhere. Who is this?"

"Laura Cantrell. From Whistler, Idaho."

"I remember," I said. "Both you and your gun."

She chuckled. "It was a very small gun, Riordan. They only seem big when they're pointed at you. Anyway, I wondered whether you found Larry Kramer?"

"Not a trace," I said. "Why?"

"I found out something today I thought you should know. Tracy, the girl that Kramer was seeing, made a phone call from here after you left. I don't know why she thought I wouldn't find out about it. When I did, I confronted her with it. She said that a man who came in with Kramer one night took her aside and said that he knew she was Kramer's special girl. He gave her a hundred dollars to call him if anything unusual happened with Kramer, if he ever talked about leaving his job, or if anybody came around asking questions about him. The man said she'd get another hundred dollars for every phone call she made about Kramer."

"How long ago was this?"

"She's not sure. At least three months ago."

"What did this man look like?"

"Big and tough, Tracy said. White-haired, so he must have been older."

"Have you got the phone number?"

She gave it to me. It was a Seattle area number.

"Laura, thanks. I don't know what this means yet, but it could mean a lot. This is the first break I've had."

"I'm glad I could help. I like you, Riordan, though I'm damned if I know why."

"Tell me, do you ever come to Seattle?"

"About once a month or so. My broker is there, and I

like the shops. Funny, I never buy much. The prices are terrible."

"The next time you're here, would you have dinner with me?"

She chuckled in a low voice. Her soft drawl thickened just slightly. "Riordan, are you asking me for a date?"

"Yes."

She laughed again and said, "Thank you for the best offer I've had in weeks. But I've got sort of a long-running understanding with a vet who lives in Missoula. We own a ranch together out in the Gallatin Valley. It'll be paid off next year, and that's when we'll get married."

"I understand. Good luck, Laura."

"Matthew, I hope I've helped. But," she added in a voice that was suddenly sober, "I don't like this mess, whatever it is. I'd like to be around long enough to live on my ranch."

"I'll try to keep you out of it. I have so far, pretty much. Be well, okay?" She thanked me and rang off. I slowly hung up the phone, thinking that there was a Missoula horse doctor who should know how lucky he really was. Then I opened another beer and dialed the telephone number that Laura Cantrell had given me.

A young woman answered. "American Freedom Foundation," she said.

CHAPTER 13

Childer's is the sort of restaurant that's hard to find these days. The businessman's lunch is usually bourbon and a half-pound rare steak that would make a cardiologist blanch and run for cover. Fifteen years ago it had been the home away from home of Seattle businessmen and baseball players, the best food and talk in the city. Now it was half empty at the height of the lunch-hour rush, an ancient relic of the absent age of the stout businessman and the expense account lunch.

I paused in the entryway and let my eyes adjust to the dim cool light of the cavernous barroom. A quiet group of lunchtime drinkers had gathered at the bar. They were late-middle-aging and expensively dressed. They listened to each other's old stories with quiet good humor, even though they had no doubt heard each story a thousand times before. The bar was their refuge from the younger men and women who talked of interfaces and team meetings and client awareness, a place where they were still listened to with respect. There is a group like that in every decent old bar in the country. Every year their numbers get smaller.

I gave my name to an elderly maître d' who shuffled me into the dining room, to Simon Blakelee's booth. Pat Miller had arranged the meeting and was already there. I kissed her lightly. She controlled her anger with me and smiled back.

Simon Blakelee sat at his regular table like an old soldier, sipping whiskey and wearing the dusty khaki safari jacket that was his trademark, a desert rat oddity in a rain-soaked city. He was a stocky man of over seventy with flowing white hair above a reddened, sun-cracked face.

Blakelee had been a courthouse and city hall reporter in Seattle for more than forty years. He knew all the important politicians and those who just thought they were important, which is to say all the rest. For the last fifteen years he had written a three-times-weekly column on politics that cut bluntly through the prevailing horseshit like a shovel. Blakelee was hard-edged and cynical, with a nose that could detect the first faint odor of corruption that arose as once honest politicians began to go bad.

He got to his feet like a fat husky dog rearing up on his hind legs, and we shook hands. "I'm Matthew Riordan," I said.

"Course you are," he rumbled in reply. "I used to see you in a couple of newsroom bars with Patricia here." He turned to the old waiter. "Mr. Riordan is a bourbon drinker, Benny. Bring him the best you've got. This is my party."

"Thanks," I replied.

"Don't mention it. Nice to see younger people in here with us old dinosaurs. Cigarette?"

"I've pretty much given them up."

He took a pack of Marlboros from his pocket and lit

one. "Then I'll smoke it. I'm too old to get cancer, anyway." He blew out some smoke and said, "Pat tells me you're looking into the disappearance of her brother."

"Among other things. I was also working for Montana Pacific, looking for one of their employees. He went missing about the same time as Pat's brother did. I still haven't found him. I got fired."

"Any connection?"

"I don't know. It's possible. I keep looking at somebody on the side of the case. Or maybe the middle. He runs the American Freedom Foundation. His name's Wilbur Hayes."

"Oh, hell, yes. Wilbur." He dragged on his cigarette and stubbed it out. "The label 'son of a bitch' was invented for Wilbur Hayes. What do you want to know?"

"Background. A history, maybe."

His old eyes gleamed. "What've you got to trade?"

"Nothing right now. But if I find anything, I'll owe you."

"Fair enough. And Pats is a friend. Anyway," he sighed, "it's hard to know where to start. I met Hayes in Korea, in '52. He was a young company commander then. Hard as hell, but his troops liked him. He knew when the book was stupid and when it wasn't and acted accordingly. So to me he seemed like a pretty good guy back then. After Korea he bounced around. Went to Nam from '66 to '70. Commanding at Fort Lewis when he retired in '72. He stayed in the area, tried a couple different businesses. None of them worked. He was pretty near broke when he started the America Freedom Foundation."

"When was that?"

"Oh, maybe 1974. After King and Kennedy were shot, and Ford nearly got it, gun control laws were being passed around the country, and that's what the foundation was started to fight. Hayes got a mailing list and a couple of typewriters and was in business. The foundation got a lot of press after a state gun control law was finally passed here in 1975. Hayes had mounted a pretty impressive fight against it. Then he branched out into the usual right-wing issues—school busing, prayer in schools, fluoridation, anything that kept the money coming in.''

"Was he ever in trouble? A lot of those foundations have had tax problems.''

"Yes, during the mid-seventies. His books were a mess. The United States attorney we had then didn't love Wilbur, and Hayes got indicted for tax fraud. He had a big defense fund, you know, government persecuting man who upholds the ideals of our Founding Fathers.'' Blakelee sipped his bourbon and made a face. "What a prick. He ended up pleading *nolo* to one count and did a half year down at Lompoc Federal Prison and Country Club for the white of collar.''

"What's he doing now?''

"You know, that's not a bad question. The foundation runs itself. Computerized mailing list of the faithful, steady givers, hired guns to testify about this bill or that in the legislature. His books are clean as mountain ice these days. Wilbur draws a pretty good salary, but I wonder if it even covers his expenses. He lives like some kind of damn prince out past Woodinville, in the horse country.''

"Is he politically connected?''

"Oh, hell yes. Ever since that idiot actor got elected, Wilbur's ideas seem pretty mainstream, pretty tame. The conservative types east of the lake drop in pretty regularly to seek his blessing. But he's smart, never endorses anybody publicly. That way the right-wing bastards with black coal for souls can get his money and his help without looking like anything but nice, clean-cut middle-of-the-roaders when they run for local office. Hayes looks like he's isolated out on the right, but he isn't. He carries much more power than anybody thinks.''

Lunch arrived, and Blakelee declared an immediate moratorium on business. He and Pat gossiped about the sexual preferences and likely life expectancy of the new managing editor of their paper. I listened with half an ear and thought about Wilbur Hayes.

There was no real evidence connecting Hayes to either Scott Griggs or Larry Kramer. Griggs's connection to the foundation was probably accidental, or at most he might be using the foundation for his own plans. It didn't seem possible that Hayes himself would be involved with any really far-out right-wing or neo-Nazi groups. The old issues of the far right—school prayer, gun control, abortion— were now planted squarely in mainstream politics, as Blakelee had said. I had read that the success of the new right's cause was cutting into the take for slick fund-raisers like Hayes. But he had nothing to gain and everything to lose by moving to the extreme fringe.

When the coffee came Blakelee had the waiter leave the pot on the table. He poured for everyone, then lit a cigarette and leaned back against the dark red leather of the banquette. He looked at me through a veil of smoke.

"Any last questions, brother?"

"A couple. The first thing is that you sound pretty ambivalent about Hayes. When you called him a son of a bitch, you almost smiled. Why is that?"

The old man's eyes narrowed. "Pretty good, kid," he said finally. "Pretty good. Yeah, I like Wilbur. Been drinking with him a time or two over the years. Wilbur's got charm. He can be a great woolly bear with a kid's wide smile. Not many people have charm, Riordan. I forgive a lot for that."

"Has there been a lot to forgive?"

Blakelee laughed. His laugh was whiskey and gravel, in equal parts. "You must be confusing me with somebody else," he said finally. "I ain't in the forgiveness business.

But I think I know what you're talking about. When he was younger Hayes raised a lot of hell. He's tossed some of the meanest fistfights in history. Tough as a board. Still is, probably.'' Blakelee stopped and coughed, the stereo rumbling hack of the heavy smoker.

I shook my head. "That's not my question. I'll be direct. Is Hayes dirty?''

Blakelee hesitated. But his answer was cold and professional. "I've never found Hayes to be worthy of trust. I don't like his opinions, never have, but there's some other right-wing politicians I know of who seem to be honorable men. With Hayes, for all his charm, I don't get that. There's a big empty spot in him where his heart and his conscience ought to be. And I wasn't kidding about the fights. The man can be violent. Brutal.'' He stopped, working over a half-formed thought. "I've heard one other thing, kind of odd. Couldn't say if it was true. But some people have said that Hayes fancies himself as some kind of Roman warrior.''

"What does that mean?''

"He's bisexual. When he's at home, he likes women. In battle, he always takes a young boy with him. That sort of Roman.''

Blakelee's words hung in the air. He finished the last of his coffee, then hauled his bulk out of the booth. "Enough of this armchair bullshit,'' he said, standing. "I got a column to get out.'' He strode away, ravaged lungs wheezing, an old soldier determined to die in battle.

I paid the bill, and then Pat and I followed him out into the sunlight.

CHAPTER 14

The Reverend Ellis Dickinson had a history that was long and honorable. He had marched with King in Selma and Memphis, been clubbed by the Chicago police while pleading for peace in Lincoln Park in 1968, and named by President Carter as an Undersecretary of Education in 1977. He was a small neat man dressed in a slightly fraying suit of clerical black. His face was broad and brown, rather than black, folded and creased by time, if not by care. He seemed filled by an inner peace, as though without any sin, except maybe pride. I was pretty sure that that would be forgiven him.

Dickinson was a lawyer, an adjunct professor of law and justice at the University of Washington, as well as the minister of the Mission Baptist Church. We met in his office on the seventh floor of the University of Washington Law School. The law building is in the university's lower campus area, just north of Portage Bay. It's a brutally modern, eight-story slab of blunt gray concrete, built in the early 1970s. The memories of student riots must have still been vivid in the mind of the university's architect.

The few windows in the building were covered by concrete screens, broken only by narrow slits to let in light. As I walked up from the parking lot, I could almost see in my mind the National Guard rifles poking out of those slits. The winds of the old days.

Dr. Dickinson's office was a shoebox of white plaster, gray concrete, and gray linoleum tile, set along a gloomy corridor of faculty offices. Dickinson had brightened the place with books and a collection of African tribal rugs in bright, strong colors. They helped.

"Unique building," I said. "I've been in more cheerful prisons."

He laughed, showing strong yellow teeth. "I tell my students it's good for them, because this is the sort of building where their clients may live for months, or years," he replied. "It impresses upon them the seriousness of their work. Now, what can I do for you? You said your inquiry had to do with the Washington Council against Racism, of which I am a member."

"I'm interested in finding out about some of the far-right political groups active in the Pacific Northwest."

"Any particular one? We have a lot. The LaRouche people, the Klan, the Posse Comitatus, the Duck Club, The Order."

"Mainly the neo-Nazi groups, The Order and the White Nations Church of God."

"If you don't mind my asking, what's the basis of your interest? Do you wish to join the council, or assist its work?"

"I might, but right right now I have a specific problem. A client has asked me to locate her brother. I found that he had joined the White Nations Church, and that he might be involved in related criminal activity. I'm hoping that with more information I can find a way to get him out of trouble, before he gets deeper into these groups."

"I see." He took a pipe from a rack on his desk and began to play with it. "Of course, you can't tell me much more than that because of your duty to your client. I hope I can help you."

"Whatever you can tell me would be helpful."

He nodded again. "Both the groups you mentioned— The Order, and the White Nations 'Church'—are splinter groups from a larger group called the Aryan Nations, in Hayden Lake, Idaho. The Order was paramilitary and clearly dangerous. As you probably have read, most of its members have been tried and convicted for conspiracy involving several bank robberies, assaults on FBI agents, and the murder of Alan Berg, the Denver radio talk show host who had denounced them.

"The White Nations 'Church' is somewhat different. Its leader, Robert Birdsall, had a falling-out with the leader of the Aryan Nations church, but they both have the same basic theology, known as Christian Identity. This belief basically holds that whites in America are God's chosen people, who must build a new Zion for whites only, and ultimately fight at the battle of Armageddon to preserve white racial purity. This belief was really founded in California, in the early 1960s. But its proponents are moving to the Pacific Northwest because it is the most 'white' area of the country."

"Why have they adopted so many Nazi trappings?" I asked. "The uniforms, the salutes, all of that nonsense."

"The Nazi regalia, however repugnant we find it, has an attraction for many people. It gives these movements a historical context, and perhaps gives them hope that they can someday prevail. Beyond the symbolic value, these people really do share the Nazi beliefs in white supremacy, 'Aryan' genetics, and so forth. Like the old Nazis, they believe that Jews control the nation's financial institutions.

These people believe that Jews use this control to promote Communism and the 'mongrelization,' or mixing, of the races.'' He sighed and tapped his empty pipe on the desk top, then put it away. "You know, one of the saddest things I have seen in recent years is the split between blacks and Jews. Groups like these hate us both, but you have extremists like Farrakhan who will make common cause with these groups in order to advance themselves.''

"That problem is a little too global for me to handle,'' I said. ''Staying strictly with these local groups, are they dangerous?''

"You're asking me to define danger, Mr. Riordan, which is something I can't do.''

"Your opinion, then.''

He took a second pipe from a rack on his desk and absently scratched it across his jaw, a man too polite to force his vices on someone else. "Opinion. They are not going to overthrow the government. They are probably not even a danger to public order, in the sense that a dozen FBI agents and, perhaps, a company of National Guardsmen could clean out their headquarters pretty thoroughly. But that's not how I define danger, sir. No.

"The danger exists in small but very real ways. These groups are led, in part, by people who are very shrewd in the handling and use of power. They prey on people who are vulnerable, be it a mental illness, depression, the loss of a farm, a job, or a girlfriend. When people are hurting, the far-right group moves in with money, friends, support. That is how they recruit. Not unlike some of the cult religions, such as the Unification Church.

"Vulnerable people are dangerous. They want to repay that support. So they become willing, perhaps much more willing, to commit crimes at the behest of the leader.

"What you end up with are gangs, like this White

Nations group, that can terrorize a small community. In the most extreme cases the terror becomes real danger. Surely you recall that a Seattle attorney and his family were killed last year by a borderline psychotic who had had his head filled with that idiotic notion that the lawyer was a dangerous Communist."

When Dickinson finished, I said, "I understand what you're saying, I think. You're equating the danger level of these groups to the danger posed by a street or biker gang."

"That's about right in the short run. But more dangerous in the long run because of the political implications. These people bring their children into their schemes, and indoctrinate them. Those children, in turn, harass and fight with other children, children of color. And so the cycle of hate continues."

He looked out his window at Portage Bay, with the rooftops of Capitol Hill in the distance. "A grim discussion for such a nice afternoon," he said. Then he smiled. "I would much rather talk to you about the healing power of God's love."

I grinned back at him. "I'm not a religious man, but if anyone could persuade me, I think you could. I have one or two more questions."

"Go ahead. My seminar starts at four, though."

"This won't take long. I'm wondering if there is any connection between these very far right groups and the American Freedom Foundation."

Dickinson frowned. "I've never heard of one. Frankly, I don't believe there would be. Wilbur Hayes is very conservative, but no one's ever accused him of being a Nazi. And if you want my personal opinion, Hayes is in the business for the money, Mr. Riordan. His fund-raising programs are very, very lucrative." He shrugged. "Beyond that I don't know."

"That's all I have, Professor. Thanks for your time."

"Not at all. And if you find this missing boy, let me know. There are counseling programs I work with that might well help."

"Thank you, I will. You've been a great help."

He stood up and showed me out, grasping my hand firmly as I stood at the door.

"Be careful, Mr. Riordan," he said. "Don't underestimate these people. Hate can make them very, very strong."

CHAPTER 15

The American Freedom Foundation had its offices in a campuslike office park of cedar-and-glass low-rise buildings between the Seattle suburbs of Bellevue and Redmond. You entered the park through a gated entrance on the highway and parked off to one side. The offices themselves looked out onto a central green lawn, showing only windowless back walls to the outside. The developers had kept a few of the original cedars and firs to shade the jogging path that wound around the perimeter, next to the redwood fence that surrounded the entire complex. Most architects say you can find out a lot about people by the kind of buildings they live and work in. If that was true, out in the suburbs they were circling the wagons and getting ready for the worst.

The American Freedom Foundation office was in the center building of the complex. The office receptionist, a blond woman of perhaps twenty, wore a demure khaki dress. She sat at a reproduction of a nineteenth-century oak library table, beneath a copy of Charles Wilson Peale's portrait of George Washington. On her table she had a small telephone PBX, a leather-bound appointment ledger, and nothing else.

"I'm Matthew Riordan," I said. "I have an appointment with Mr. Hayes at ten-thirty."

"Yes, sir," she replied. "It will be about twenty minutes. Please sit down, and help yourself to our journal, *The Freedom Letter*." She spoke mechanically, like a well-rehearsed puppet. I sat down.

The Freedom Letter was really jazzy. The four-color cover showed a picture of Wilbur Hayes sitting at a conference table on a stage with a motley group of right-wing political and religious mugwumps, an enormous American flag hanging on the wall behind them. The inside pages were printed on slick paper. I looked at the contents page. In one issue, I could learn about the dangers of gun control, the evil of abortion, the Gestapo tactics of the IRS, and the overwhelming demand of little children for the right to pray and hold religion classes in the public schools. I could also send my check to defeat godless liberals in the upcoming congressional elections, to keep struggling religious broadcasters with wavy pompadour haircuts on television, or buy supplies for the Somocistas in Nicaragua. Excuse me. Freedom fighters.

I was still learning about this New American Way when the appointed moment came and Wilbur Hayes stepped into the lobby. Hayes was big, an inch or two over my six foot three, with the bulky upper body of a hard-muscled man in late middle age. His face was strong and blunt, with a long thick nose, square jaw, and small bright blue eyes. His hair was grayish-white, still thick on top, shaved Army close on the sides.

Hayes mangled my hand with what passed for a handshake and ushered me into his office. "Sit down, sit down, Mr. Riordan," he said pleasantly.

Hayes parked himself in a tufted leather chair behind

about half an acre of mahogany desk. I looked closely at
him as he shuffled together the papers he had been working on.

At first glance he looked like the cliché of the New
Right hustler I expected him to be, but there were subtle
signs of complexity beneath the surface. Hayes was, for all
his thick-muscled power, given to little hints of elegance—
manicured nails, hand-tailored suits, a bit of a curl in the
hair on top of his head, above the close-cropped sides. I
had a sudden vision of Hayes as a 1930s child shown in an
old photograph, a child in a sailor suit with long curly
hair. It was bizarre, but it stuck.

Hayes's voice snapped me out of my reverie.

"Cigar, Mr. Riordan?" he asked.

"No, thanks."

"Hope you don't mind if I do," he said. He selected a
slender five-inch panatela and lit it, contentedly puffing
blue smoke. "Jamaican," he said. "From Cuban seed and
pretty good, but somehow just not the same. It'd almost be
worth trading with that Castro bastard just to get a fine
cigar again. Ah, well," he said, smiling, "you aren't here
to talk cigars. Over the phone yesterday you said you were
a lawyer. What can I do for you?"

"Provide a little information, I hope. A friend of mine
has asked me to help her look for her younger brother, a
man named Keith Miller. He's about twenty-two now, but
this is the most recent photograph I have." I passed a copy
of Keith's graduation picture across the desk to Hayes. He
studied it briefly, his face blank. He passed it back and
said, "I'm afraid I don't know this young man. Should
I?"

"Not necessarily. Miller seems to have been friends
with another man, Scott Alan Griggs. I did some checking
on Griggs' background. He worked for you until about
four months ago."

"Yes, I remember Scott Griggs. A fine man. He worked as a security guard for me, I believe."

"If you don't mind my asking, why did Griggs quit working for you?"

"I don't mind, son, but I'm not sure I know the exact reason. Scott said he didn't much like living in the city, wanted to get back to the country. I can understand that. Me and my horses, we live as far away from town and my ex-wife as we can." He smiled at his small joke.

"Were you aware that Griggs was convicted of armed robbery?"

Hayes grunted softly and took the cigar out of his mouth. He leaned forward in his chair, face reddening slightly. "Yes, I was. Griggs was a Vietnam vet who had trouble coming home. He made some mistakes, and he paid society back for them. Now," he added softly, but with a crack in his voice, "just what the hell makes it your business, mister?"

"My friend is concerned about her brother, that's all," I said mildly. "Her brother started palling around with Griggs a few months ago, and they apparently joined the White Nation Church of God shortly afterwards. I'm asking you questions about Griggs because you employed him and have a lot of contacts in the, uh, conservative circles. That makes you a long shot, but a logical one."

Hayes shook his head in amazement, a superior grin across his face. "Riordan, you don't honestly believe that I agree with the neo-Nazi groups up in Idaho, do you?"

"I don't know what to believe about you, Colonel Hayes."

"Well then let me set you straight, damn it." He pointed the cigar at me and poked the air with it. "My group fights for what made this country great, a belief in God, prayer, the right to bear arms in defense of home and family, fighting crime. We don't support forced mixing of the races, but we're not some hate group. Hell, I commanded black soldiers and Jews and Puerto Ricans and some boys I'd swear came from another planet. And I never held their race against them.'' He stopped and paused for breath, pulsing with indignation.

"I'm not accusing you of anything, Mr. Hayes. I'm just trying to find a missing kid.''

"Well, I just wanted to set the record straight with you, Riordan.''

"I understand. I have just a few more questions.'' I handed him a photograph of Larry Kramer and told him a lie. "I don't know who this man is, but he may have had some dealings with Miller and Griggs. He was seen with them.''

He looked at the photograph carefully. His eyes widened slightly. "Where did you get that information?'' he asked.

"I really can't say, sir. You recognize this man, then?''

"Damn it, I didn't say that. Quit putting words in my mouth.''

"I'm not, I'm just wondering what your interest in this man is.''

"I don't have any interest, Riordan,'' he said, annoyed. "I've never seen this man before.'' He flipped the picture back across his desk to me. As I reached for it a corner of the picture caught on the air and the photo skittered to the floor. I reached down and picked it up. As I straightened again I saw Hayes smiling, as though he had won some kind of childish battle. Maybe he had. He wasn't taking the bait. I tried again.

"Ever travel to northern Idaho, Mr. Hayes?'' I asked breezily.

"Sometimes, I suppose,'' he said, taken aback by the off-the-wall question.

"I'm told there's a good hotel in Whistler. The Silver

Bow Hotel. I'm told it has some unusual services. Have you ever stayed there, Mr. Hayes?''

"I don't know what you're talking about."

"Surely you've been by the place, Mr. Hayes. It's right on Zinc Street. There's a girl named Tracy there. She works the door. And the telephones.''

Hayes stared at me, his eyes narrowed into slits.

"What's the game we're playing here, Riordan?'' he asked. "I don't mind playing games. I'm a soldier and a gambler. But I like to know the game, and the rules.''

"There's no game, Colonel Hayes. And no rules. This is your office, and I'm taking up your time. You can do what you want. I'm just asking some questions.''

"Sure you are, Riordan,'' he said heavily. "Sure.'' He chuckled to himself. "I suspect you're pretty good at playing these kinds of games too. Were you ever a soldier?''

"Not much of one.''

"Just curious. The greatest authority on the strategy of war—war is the greatest of games—was a Chinese soldier, a general, Sun Tzu. He probably lived in about the third century before Christ. I memorized some of his sayings when I was a young officer. A couple have stayed in my mind through all these years. The one that sticks out the most is this one: 'There are some roads not to follow; some troops not to strike, some cities not to assault; and some ground which should not be contested.' ''

I said, "So?''

"So nothing. I've got to get back to work, Riordan. Sorry I can't help you.'' He got up and opened the door.

As I passed him in the doorway I began to doubt whether I knew the game, or the rules.

CHAPTER 16

The fact that Wilbur Hayes had lied about knowing Keith Miller and Larry Kramer didn't help me very much. It wasn't something the Seattle police or the Montana Pacific people would get very excited about. The cops know that most people involved in a criminal investigation will lie to protect themselves, or protect someone else. Many will lie for fun. A few will even lie for free.

On Thursday morning, two days after seeing Wilbur Hayes, I sat in my office trying to figure out what the hell to do next. I spent most of the morning working on that question. The best answer I kept coming up with was lunch. Then the phone rang. It was Bernstein.

"I'm at the Orchard Tavern, in Oronodo," he said without preamble. "It's a one-street town on the east side of the Columbia, north of Wenatchee."

"Terrific," I said. "How is it?"

"The hamburgers are lousy but the beer is cold. Pay attention, shithead. I've been working. I picked up Griggs in Sandpoint, Idaho, yesterday. I've been on him ever since. He's holed up in a farmhouse about three miles east of the Columbia on Highway 2. He's got Keith Miller with him.''

"That's good," I said. "But why are you doing this? I thought you wanted no part of Miller."

"I don't care about Miller," he replied. "I want the others. If you and Patty want to try and get her little brother's ass out before I light up a fire, that's fine with me. But get over here now. These bastards are up to something, and I want to know what it is."

"Okay," I said quickly. "Where do we meet? At the tavern?"

"Don't be stupid. I've got to be able to watch the house. Take Highway 2 out two and a half miles from Orondo. There will be a gravel road on your right. I think it's Badger Mountain Road, but I'm not sure. It heads up in the coulees above the river. I'll be about a mile or so up the road. Move it." He hung up.

I called Patty at the *Post*. "Bernstein's found your brother," I said when she came on the line. "He's over by the Columbia River, east of the mountains. Bernstein wants us to get over there. Can you leave?"

"Absolutely."

"Good. Meet me at my house in a half hour, no more. Jeans or wool pants, hiking boots, and a down jacket for the night. It'll be cold in the mountains."

"What are we going to do when we get there?"

"I don't know," I admitted, and hung up the phone.

Patty drove her Porsche hard, blowing past the slow-moving campers and station wagons on steep and narrow Highway 2. We crossed Stevens Pass in well under two hours, and made Wenatchee in under three. We crossed the Columbia on the bridge above Rocky Reach Dam and turned north, following the river. At Orondo, sixteen miles upriver, Highway 2 turned away from the river to the east to cross the sun-scorched lava plains of eastern Washington. When the road turned away from the river, I cleared the trip odometer to clock the 2.5 inland miles and began to watch for the road that Bernstein had told me of.

It was there as promised, with a small metal sign beside it that read "Badger Mountain Ski Area." Patty downshifted the Porsche and swept onto the narrow road. The asphalt pavement was old and broken up. She didn't slow down much. I glanced over at her as she fought to hold the car on the road. Fine thin lines of determination creased her face.

We found Bernstein downhill from the road, seated beneath a shrubby larch, a bottle of beer by his side and field glasses pressed against his face. He had parked his truck up the road, behind a screen of ponderosa pines. Patty parked the Porsche near his truck. Together we jogged back down the road.

"They're still in there," Bernstein said as we approached. "But a good-sized panel truck pulled up about fifteen minutes ago. Nothing on or off it so far."

"How do you know they're still in there?"

Bernstein took the field glasses away from his face and gave me a withering look.

"Excuse me," I said. "Stupid question."

"Damn straight. They got here late last night. One other guy was here already, but he checked out early this morning, like he was going to work. I couldn't see him well enough to tell if he was one of the clowns at the White Morons Church or not."

"I want to go down and talk to Keith," Patty said.

Bernstein half turned toward her. He was still sitting down. "No," he said. "If they're armed like they were at the church, they'd shoot your ass off before you got within a hundred yards of the door. Which would be a shame."

Patty kicked him in the back.

"So what do we do now?" Patty asked.

"We wait. You guys bring any food?"

"No," Patty said. "Yes," I said. "Crackers and hard salami and cheese and a couple of six-packs. I was in a hurry."

Bernstein smiled and handed Patty the field glasses. "Should have married the man, Pats," he said. "He'd probably do the laundry, too."

Patty took over watching the truck. Bernstein ate. He took me aside when he had finished. "You bring a piece?"

"No. I didn't think I'd need one."

"Think again. It's okay, I can supply."

"Patty wants Keith in one package," I said. "Still breathing."

"Do my best. But Matthew, before you get too wrapped up in who he is, remember *what* he is."

I was silent. Bernstein refuses to lie to himself. And he won't lie to other people.

"Hey!" Patty hissed. "Movement down there."

I took over the glasses. Four men were walking out of the house. They paused on the front porch to pull on jackets and lace up boots. One man threw away a cigarette, its coal tracing a glowing arc in the gathering dusk. The four men climbed into the truck. The truck grumbled into life and began to back out of the farmyard.

"Did you see Keith?" Patty demanded.

"Couldn't tell," I replied. "He might have been the one off to the right."

"Let's go," Bernstein commanded. "We've got to pick them up before they hit the river, see which way they go."

We caught up to the panel truck just before it reached the river at Orondo. The truck turned north on State 151 and followed the river. It crossed the Columbia at Chelan and turned north again on Highway 97.

"They're heading for the Manzanita Valley," I said. "I

don't know why that makes sense, but it does. Somehow this thing fits in with the missing Larry Kramer, and he went missing from there. But how does it fit?"

"That's what we're going to find out," Bernstein replied.

For the next hour Bernstein played a delicate game of tag with the panel truck, speeding up or slowing down to change the distance between his truck and the truck in front of us, playing with his pickup's lights, sometimes driving with lights off. The night was clear, with bright starlight and a half-moon lighting the sky. The peaks of the Okanogan range were silhouetted like black-burned cathedrals against the dark blue sky.

A mile past Darien the panel truck's brake lights flashed and it swung off the highway onto a gravel Forest Service road. Bernstein switched off his own lights and pulled to the side of the highway.

"Where does that road go?" Bernstein demanded.

"I think it goes over Goat Pass," I replied. "But it doesn't connect to anything, because the other side of the pass is in the national park."

"Any branch roads?"

"If I remember the maps in the Montana Pacific office, there's just one. The rest are logging roads. It's dry tonight, but they'd still have a tough time driving that truck on the logging roads."

"Who owns this land?"

"It's mostly Forest Service land, but the Montana Pacific has some pretty big inholdings, along with other private landowners. In fact, the branch road turns southwest, toward the White Rose ski area site."

"We'll give them about a mile head start, then gradually close it. With luck they won't see our dust plume."

We waited. The truck was out of sight on the Forest Service road. Bernstein followed, driving without lights.

The road was bad, scattered with loose rock and still cut

up by gullies opened up in last spring's runoff. Bernstein gritted his teeth and did the best he could without lights, but we dropped farther behind the panel truck.

Three or four miles up the road we came to the single fork. The panel truck wasn't in sight. Not even a dust cloud remained to point which way the truck had gone.

"I think," Bernstein said tightly, "that I have fucked up. Which way, the lady or the tiger?"

"Left," I said firmly. "Toward the ski area."

"Why?" Pats asked.

"I'm following a hunch. The ski area is the only thing that ties these people to Larry Kramer. Hell, I could be wrong, but I'm not uncertain."

"Good enough," Bernstein said. He took the left fork.

We crawled along the gravel road, lights out. Less than two miles down the left fork we felt the metallic rumble of a railroad crossing beneath the pickup. "Slow down," I said to Bernstein. "We're close."

Then we got lucky. From the top of the next rise the land fell away in a gently sloping, bowl-shaped valley. At the far edge of the bowl, dimly visible in the moonlight, there was a gravel pit scraped out of the valley like an open wound. The panel truck was backed up to the edge of the pit.

"All right, sports fans," Bernstein said. "Main event coming up."

He pulled the pickup into a small clearing by the side of the road, edging as far into the brushy second-growth timber as he could. We got out of the truck on the passenger side, away from the woods. As he slid out of the truck Bernstein paused and reached under the dash. He pulled out a flat, squarish automatic and handed it to me. I pulled the clip and checked the action. It was a 7.65-mm Walther PPK.

"Very nice," I said. "You start shopping where James Bond does?"

"Got it in a card game down in Taos. But don't lose it. It's clean and is presently registered to a fellow in Albuquerque whose tombstone has been voted straight Democrat for every ticket since Humphrey-Muskie in '68."

Patty's eyes widened when she saw the gun. "No," she hissed. "Not while my brother's there."

Bernstein took Patty gently by both arms. His voice was patient. "Look, Pats, cut the shit. We'll try not to hurt your brother. But face facts. This isn't going to be a nice family reunion. Those creeps your brother has taken to hanging out with would kill a nice lady liberal like you in a minute." To me he added, "We stay in the woods. If we move diagonally down this ridge, we should wind up across the gravel pit from them, and be able to see them pretty clearly."

"Sounds good," I replied. "Let's go."

We walked quietly through the trees. From the maps I had seen I thought we were near the ski area site, still on national forest or private land, not in the national park. The woods were logged over, heavy with trashy undergrowth. Sometimes we walked past the stumps of the old-growth trees, ponderosa pines and grand firs that once had stood there a hundred feet tall.

It took us almost half an hour to cover the mile across the ridge to the edge of the gravel pit. We crouched behind a car-sized boulder outcropping fifty yards uphill from the edge of the pit and waited.

The truck was about a hundred fifty yards away, across the gravel pit. Two of the men stood watch, one on each side of the truck, rifles cradled in their arms. The other two men unloaded drums from the back of the truck and tipped them over, dumping their contents into the pit.

We could hear them a little. Their words drifted to us on

the light night wind. One of the men swore as a drum slipped from his grasp as he dumped it. He stood up and called out, "Hey Pierce, change places. I'm getting tired," as he walked toward the guards.

Patty gasped when she heard the voice. "That's Keith," she whispered.

One of the guards handed his rifle to Keith Miller and walked toward the back of the truck. Miller slung the rifle over his shoulder and lit a cigarette, the match flaring in the dark. The other guard must have seen it. He walked around the truck and knocked the cigarette out of Miller's mouth, stamping on it while cussing Miller like a Marine Corps drill instructor.

"That sounds like Griggs," I whispered.

Bernstein nodded.

"What are they doing?" Patty said.

"Probably dumping something," Bernstein answered. "Disposing of hazardous chemicals properly is expensive. Midnight dumping is cheaper. So if you have a business that creates a lot of highly toxic waste and you don't want to take the risk of dumping it yourself, you let the contract to a bunch of creeps like these."

Patty said. "Oh, shit. That stupid jerk."

Bernstein had his field glasses to his eyes. "They're finishing up, I think," he said. "Wait. One guy is climbing up the ridge to that old mine entrance."

"What's up there?"

"I don't know. When they leave we can find out."

CHAPTER 17

We made our way carefully down the ridge to the gravel pit. The moonlight was still pretty good, but the ground was broken, and in high country you don't want to get overconfident. This was not a good time to snap an ankle. Or to have that truck come back, for that matter.

The pit was years, maybe decades old. Its edges had collapsed and eroded into a slope covered with scrub. Gravel had been taken more recently from the center and the far edge of the pit. We walked into the pit, loose gravel from the newly mined area sometimes moving under our feet. It felt a little like walking on the moon.

Bernstein walked in the lead, his automatic drawn. When he reached the area where the barrels had been dumped he stopped. He scooped some gravel up in his hand.

"It's oily," he said. He didn't raise his voice, but it filled the mountain stillness. He rubbed his fingers together and sniffed them. "Refined oil, like diesel or number-two fuel oil."

"Don't do that," I said quickly. "Wipe your hands off and throw the rag away."

"Why?"

"Lots of things get dissolved in light oil. Insecticides like 2,4,5-T or parathion. PCBs."

Bernstein wiped his hands on his bandanna, quickly. He threw the cloth away.

We backed away from the area where the oil had been dumped and scrambled out of the pit. We were now halfway between the ridge where we had waited and the logging road. We walked, following the edge of the pit, in a half circle toward the road.

A few yards farther on Bernstein stopped and pulled a flashlight out of the daypack he carried like a hump between his broad shoulders. He shone the light. A deep track from a heavyweight tire had been cut into the ground.

"They've been dumping here for quite a while, I think," Bernstein said.

"Well, they're not dumping oil to jack up prices for OPEC," I replied. "The oil's got to be contaminated."

"But why are they dumping it here?" Patty asked. "I thought there were disposal sites for hazardous waste."

"There are," I said. "A few, that are properly licensed and can meet the new federal standards for incineration of liquids and for safe landfills. But there aren't very many, and even disposal sites and methods that everyone used to think were safe have proved to have problems. The few safe, approved incinerators for, say, contaminated oil are very expensive. Chemical decontamination is even more expensive. It's a lot cheaper to dump it. It's also a felony. Back east the mob has moved into the business in a big way."

"Not here?"

"I doubt it. This is not a business Henry Cruz, the Tacoma mob boss, would approve of. It's off his Pierce County turf, it probably doesn't pay enough—no more than eight or nine hundred percent profit—and for him there'd be exposure. Cruz has a healthy respect for the Justice Department, which would love to tie him to something nasty and public like this.''

''But why is Keith involved?''

''Your brother and his neo-Nazi pals are cheap labor, I'd guess. They may have gone into the business to raise money for the cause. I don't know.''

''This is interesting,'' Bernstein said impatiently, ''but I want to check out that mine and get the hell out of this valley. Just in case they decide to make a second delivery tonight.''

''Let's get going,'' Patty agreed.

We hiked around the edge of the pit to the road. The old mine entrance was on the hill above the logging road, but a steep spur road had been cut into the side of the hill to reach the mouth of the mine. There were piles of mine tailings and loose rock around the mine entrance. A tangle of rusting equipment had been shoved to one side. But the spur itself was clear.

Bernstein saw it too. ''Yeah,'' he said when I pointed it out, ''I think I could get a truck up here, if I had to.''

We trudged up the hill to the mine mouth. The entrance had been reinforced with timbers maybe fifty or sixty years before. They were sagging and cracked. It didn't look like anyone had worked the mine since the 1930s at the latest. The North Cascades are dotted with small mines like this one—silver, gold, lead, and zinc. None of them was ever a mother lode.

The air of the mine smelled both rotten and sharp. Bernstein shone his light into the mine. Inside the entrance the mine was empty, the floor dry.

''Looks all right,'' he said.

I took my flashlight out of my pack and switched it on. ''Okay,'' I said. ''Let's try it. But we can't stay long. That rotten-egg smell is probably hydrogen sulfide. I remember that much from high school chemistry. But God only knows what that sharp acid smell is."

We walked into the mine, crouching low to stay beneath the sloping rock ceiling.

The mine drove straight back into the ridge for a few yards, then curved to the right, probably following a vein of silver twisting into the mountain. The roof of the mine shaft fell lower as it turned into the mountain. Claustrophobic fear rose up in my throat. The air grew hot and more foul as we followed the shaft. Patty began to choke on the fetid air. Bernstein wet down her bandanna from his water bottle and tied it over her mouth. After that she was a little better.

The mine curved left again as the shaft opened into a gallery. The mine was totally black now. We played our flashlights off the walls to partly light the area. The gallery was half filled with fifty-five-gallon drums. None of the drums had any markings or labels. Some of them had leaked or split open, spilling a brown frothy chemical stew on the floor of the mine.

The three of us searched the gallery area as best we could. Since we had only our flashlights, the gallery was a swirl of shallow pools of moving light. My chest burned. The gasses released from the decaying barrels were starting to sear our lungs.

"Anything?" I choked out, breathing labored.

"Nothing," Patty replied. "The barrels are all unmarked, and I haven't found anything else."

"Me either," said Bernstein. "Let's get out of here."

"Okay." I circled one last time around the perimeter of the gallery, trying to make sure we hadn't overlooked anything in our search. Still nothing.

The rock wall had begun to collapse at the rear of the gallery. At the base of the crumbling wall there was a pile of loose rock from a recent fall. I passed by it without thought, shining my flashlight over it to avoid bruising a foot or a shin on a jagged rock.

A shred of black plastic stuck out from among the rocks.

"Bernstein," I said, choking out his name.

He came over quickly, moving his bulk nimbly between the barrels.

"Take a look at this."

He picked up a rock next to the scrap of plastic and set it carefully aside. I did the same.

The scrap was attached to something larger.

We pulled more rocks off the pile, working carefully in case there was something underneath. The plastic scrap was part of a larger plastic sheet, about the weight and thickness of a heavy trash bag. We kept working until we had uncovered a foot-square section of the black plastic.

Bernstein took out a belt knife and slit the plastic. He peeled it away.

Underneath the plastic was a human hand.

The hand was bloated with putrefaction until the fingers were the size of sausages. The skin had split under the gas pressure of decay.

I heard a choking sound behind me and turned to see Patty walking quickly out of the mine. I followed her. I found her on her knees just outside the mine entrance, kneeling behind a pile of tailings. She was retching. I helped her until I could stand it no longer. Then I went off to be sick myself.

When I came back, Bernstein and Pats were sitting outside the mine. Bernstein held out a camper's tin cup half filled with brandy and lukewarm water. I took it and rinsed my mouth.

We were silent. Finally Bernstein said, "You think we ought to go back and finish unwrapping him? Whoever he is?"

"No," I replied. "I haven't got the stomach for it. And I think I already know who it is."

"Who?" Patty demanded.

"A guy you don't know," I replied. "An engineer named Larry Kramer."

We hiked back to Bernstein's pickup truck in silence, each of us wrapped up in our own concerns. Patty wanted to find her brother Keith in time to protect him from the storm that was surely coming for him now that his involvement in the toxic waste dumping and murder was clear. I was trying to figure out how the killing of Larry Kramer fit in with Bernie Seaton's murder. Bernstein's emotions were more obvious. He was disappointed that he hadn't gotten the chance to kill somebody.

When we reached the truck we stopped to rest. We were all terribly hungry, after vomiting outside the mine, but the only food we had left was dry trail mix. We swallowed a little, dutifully, washed down with the last of the brandy and water. I felt a little sick, but I wasn't hungry any longer.

As we were chewing on the trail mix, Patty asked, "If it is this man Kramer's body, why did they leave it in the mine? Why not dump it someplace else?"

"They probably killed him here," Bernstein replied. "Moving him would be risky. My guess would be that they plan to dynamite the mine shut when they fill it up with waste barrels anyway."

"I just wish I knew where the hell they were working from," I said with frustration. "I don't think they'll go back to that farmhouse that Bernstein had staked out. That can't be their headquarters; it's too small to be used for collecting and shipping the chemical waste."

"I didn't find out where they were working from," Bernstein said. "But whatever we're going to do, we have to do tonight. Tomorrow we've got to report the dumping and the corpse. If the Environmental Protection Agency can get up here fast enough, maybe they can keep the stuff dumped in the gravel pit from leaching too far into the ground."

"This is going to sound silly," Patty said, "But did either of you take a good look at the truck?"

"Sure," Bernstein said. "No signs or labels. I didn't see anything else."

"Didn't you look at the mud flaps?"

"No. Why?"

"Because they said 'Apple City Transfer Company, Wenatchee, Washington.' "

CHAPTER 18

Patty and I crouched beside the rusting hulk of a '56 Ford pickup abandoned in the side lot of a boarded-up Shell station on Columbia Street in Wenatchee. The Apple City Transfer Warehouse lay across Columbia Street from our hiding place, a square two-story building of tired gray limestone rock, maybe fifty or sixty years old. The Apple City sign was weathered and peeling, the painted advertisements for Coca-Cola and Chesterfield cigarettes faded to bare outlines on the crumbling rock. The building had a false front facing the street and stretched back eighty feet or more. The offices were in front, with the truck bays on the left side of the building, big old double-hung windows on the right. It was a little after five in the morning.

I watched the sky and worried. The moon had fallen down to the west, and thin high clouds had covered the stars, turning the sky into a great high dome of murky, slightly whitened starlight. But a narrow gray line of dawn light could already be seen on the eastern horizon, across the seared brown desert hills. We had to hurry. Where in hell was Bernstein?

He stepped out from the corner of the old gas station behind us and whistled softly. Patty and I got up from our vantage point and joined him behind the station.

"I circled around so that if I got picked up nobody would find you," he said, slightly out of breath. "The truck's gone, but I've got our way in. One of the windows around the back of the building is open. We can slide it up without any trouble."

"Guards?" I asked.

"I didn't see any. Makes me wonder if this is just a wild-ass guess."

"Could be."

"You sure you and Patty want to go through with this? They might be waiting for us. And the three of us aren't exactly a SWAT team."

"I'm not sure. But you're going in there no matter what, aren't you?"

"Yes. You know why."

"Then I'm going."

Patty cut in. "We've got to try it. If Keith stays with this group, he'll never get out. If we find him, I want to get him out of there first thing," she said.

Bernstein popped a kitchen match on a thumbnail and lit a cigarette. The red glow lit up his harsh features and heavy beard. "No," he said simply. "Not unless he wants to go. This is the third time I'm telling you, Pats, and it will be the last. You seem to think your brother's the little prince held captive by the pirates. He's not. He's one of the bad guys. And I'll be damned if I'll go to jail as an accessory on a half-dozen assorted felony charges, plus murder. Not for some fucking Nazi."

"Stop calling him that," she hissed angrily. "He's just a kid. He'll listen to me once I talk to him."

"You don't know that, Pats," I said gently. "Bernstein's right. As usual. Unfortunately. We've got to face facts. The only thing you could do for Keith now, even if you got him out of there, is walk him right over to the sheriff's office and have him surrender. Anything else would be a criminal act. Accept that or stay behind."

She was quiet for a long minute. Her jawline worked and she clenched her fists in frustration, but there were no tears. Not for Patty.

"All right," she said finally, staring at Bernstein. "You're right. But don't kill him. He's what family I've got."

Bernstein nodded. "We walk down one block, cross the street, and come up the back alley. If the cops take an interest, I'm your drunk friend who can't remember where my car is. He reached inside his down vest and checked the action on his .45. I did the same. Full clip plus one in the chamber.

We came up on the building from the rear alley, staying close to the warehouse wall, outside the pools of light left by scattered streetlights. Bernstein stepped up to the corner window. The sill was about five feet off the ground. He got his fingers under the lower pane and heaved. It slid up slowly, creaking. Bernstein took out his automatic and laid it on the sill. Then he put both hands flat on the sill and boosted himself easily through the window. When he was inside, he reached back for the gun.

"Okay," he whispered from inside. "Send Patty."

I got down on one knee and laced my hands together. She scorned the offer and boosted herself through as Bernstein had. I followed. When I was inside the building, Bernstein turned back and closed the window.

It was dark. The only light leaked in through dirty windows. We crouched in the corner, waiting for our eyes to adjust to the darkness inside.

When I could see, I looked around. Most of the warehouse floor was clear. Empty pallets were stacked along the walls, between bins of framed wood and chain-link wire fencing that once might have held apples. There were four loading docks built along the far wall. Near two of the loading doors were rows of unmarked fifty-five-gallon drums, the same type we had seen in the abandoned mine.

"I think we're in the right place," Bernstein said. "Hot dog. Let's go catch these guys. I'm going to work through the place back to front. Patty, you stay with me. Matthew, go check out the offices in front, then come back."

"Okay," I said. "Keep me covered for just a minute, in case they're laying for us."

I worked my way to the front of the building, stopping behind each stack of pallets and listening for the sound of anyone waiting in the dark. It was quiet but for the thumping sound of blood pumping through my veins.

The front of the warehouse had been cut up into a warren of little offices. I moved as quietly as I could to the door of the first one. It was built of cheap sheetrock and hollow-core plywood doors. The walls would resist sound no more than air would.

I reached the first office and flattened myself along its outer wall. I turned the doorknob slowly and pushed the door open. I waited. Nothing. I slipped inside the door, gun held straight up, ready to chop down and fire.

Nothing. The office was empty, even of furniture. A rat squeaked in the corner and scampered across the floor. I jumped about three inches and nearly blew the little bastard into eternity.

When I steadied down again I saw a connecting door to the next office. I closed the door to the outside gently and went to the inner door and pushed it open.

I smelled the stale cigar smoke too late. A desk lamp across the room flicked on. I was caught, frozen in the doorway.

Wilbur Hayes sat behind a scarred wooden office desk. His broad face was shadowed by the light, his eyes hidden in their darkened sockets. He smiled like an obscene statue.

"Come on in, Riordan," he chuckled. "You've no place else to go." He pointed a .45 Army service automatic at me. The black hole of the muzzle looked as big as a tunnel.

I took two steps into the office and dropped my gun on the carpeted floor. Then I fell back against the wall like an exhausted fighter.

Hayes laughed. "What you have here, gentlemen," he said to Keith Miller and Scott Griggs, sitting beside him, "is one scared little man who's out of his depth. And who knows it."

I looked around the room. Keith Miller perched jauntily on one side of the desk, close to Hayes, almost like a child beside his father. He laughed at Hayes's comment, sneering at me like a half-assed teenager. There was going to be a killing, and he liked that. It was fun. His round moon face was bright and sharp with excitement.

Scott Griggs was a different sort of man entirely. He sat silently in a straight wooden desk chair, lean and rangy and tough. He held a smallish snub-nosed revolver in his lap loosely, almost casually. His eyes and his weathered face showed no emotion.

"Riordan's scared, but he's not dumb," Scott Griggs said. "He's not here all by himself." He eased himself out of his chair and took my gun from the floor. He put it on Hayes's desk.

"Good point," Hayes replied. "Griggs, you head outside, check around the building perimeter. If he's called in the local cops, they should be easy to spot. Keith, you check the warehouse. If you see somebody out there, don't try to take them. Come back and report."

Griggs merely nodded and slipped smoothly out. Keith Miller made a show of it. He checked the action on his automatic with exaggerated motions, like a bit player in a melodrama. He nodded at Hayes. "I'll get them, sir," he whispered. He raised his gun hand from the elbow until his weapon pointed straight up, ready to chop down. Then he slipped out through the office's side door.

I half expected Hayes, as a former combat officer, to grab Keith Miller by the scruff of the neck and shake him a bit to remind him that this was real life and not a late-night television movie starring Trevor Howard. Instead, he was smiling fondly, almost prettily. And suddenly I remembered what Simon Blakelee had said, that Hayes was rumored to go both ways.

Hayes caught me looking at him. "Keith's a good boy," he said.

"In more ways than one, I'm sure," I replied dryly.

If Hayes caught the gibe, he didn't react. I pushed on. This was a game that time would decide. And I played for it. "Tell me something, Hayes," I said. "You have money and political power and military honors. Why are you dragging yourself through the mud like this, a garbageman for criminals?"

He didn't answer right away. He stared straight ahead, into the darkness somewhere behind me. I could see him only by the small lamp on his desk, the only light in the room. The light was uneven. Where it was bright I could see his pink scalp shining through his short military haircut. But Hayes's broad, blunt face was still half hidden, unknowable, mere shifting pools of light and shadow.

"I'm in a war, Riordan," he finally said. "My third. This one I intend to win."

"A war?" I said, confused. "A war for what?"

"A war for a new nation. A white nation, here in the Northwest. One that's not controlled by Jews or that bows down in front of the blacks. This"—he gestured broadly to the rest of the warehouse—"is just a means to that end. Wars have to be financed. I've got some money, but the Jew bastards that run the IRS keep such a close watch on me that I can't use any of it."

"You're insane," I told him.

"Am I?" he said. He raised his head so that I could see his face in the lamplight. His eyes glittered like wet glass. "I'm building slowly, waiting when I have to. Our brothers in The Order wouldn't do that. They started their campaign before they were strong. And the Zionist-controlled government destroyed them."

"The Jews don't control the government."

"You're blind, Riordan. Blind. Jews have controlled the U.S. government ever since Roosevelt, that secret Jew, became our dictator. And they've stabbed us in the back in Korea, in Nicaragua, in Vietnam. Vietnam was the worst. A betrayal. I saw thousands of fine boys die in a war we weren't allowed to win. But you wouldn't know about that, would you, Riordan? You were one of the Communist punks who marched against your own people to help Hanoi, weren't you?"

"I marched," I said quietly. "At Washington and New York, and at Quang Tri and Hue and down in the Mekong Delta. I watched my friends die in a war we lost, Hayes. We lost fighting a disciplined, patient, ruthless opponent who knew the terrain and had fought for thirty years to get the foreigners out of his country. There is no shame in losing such a war. And there is no rewriting history."

"Perhaps not," Hayes admitted. "But there is a time when brave men write their own history. It only takes a few. Time will decide who is right. But you can walk away from this, Riordan, if you want to. All you have to do is leave us alone. We seek no harm to anyone. All we want is a place of our own, a place where the white race can defend itself and remain pure."

"You've already killed too many people, Hayes. We found Larry Kramer's body in the old mine above the gravel pit near Jack Pine Mountain. You or your people probably killed Bernie Seaton, too. And God knows how many cases of cancer or leukemia your chemical dumps will cause. Did you check for PCBs or radioactives in the waste you dumped, Hayes? Your crime is a large one and a long one. You may still be killing people fifty years from now.''

''In all wars there are risks. And casualties.''

Suddenly I was tired and angry beyond reason.

''Don't mouth platitudes at me, you bastard,'' I hissed. ''I'm sick of you. I'm sick of causes, of red terror and black, left and right. I'm sick of fanatics shooting or bombing innocent people in airports and train stations and churches. I'm sick of people so weak, so gutless, that they have to invent conspiracies and monsters to explain away their own failures.''

As I paused for breath I watched him. The line of his jaw tightened a little. I pushed on, harder.

''Weaklings like you, Hayes. You can tell that fable about Vietnam being a stab in the back to kids like Miller and head-cases like Griggs if you want, but don't lay it on me. I was there, and I watched candy-assed officers like you punch your tickets and do your tours up in the choppers and inside the barbed-wire perimeters of the firebases while you left the grunts to do the real fighting. None of you had any guts. You haven't got the balls to take me on right now.''

A wave of anger washed over his face. He fought it back.

''Keith will be back soon,'' he said. ''Then we'll shut your mouth.''

I laughed harshly. ''You're fucking him, aren't you? I've heard the rumors that you do boys. Keith's not coming back, Hayes. I've got a man outside who can slit the throat of a moron like Keith without breaking a sweat. Then you'll be all alone. Just another aging queen.''

The game was working.

It was a mistake.

Hayes exploded from behind the desk. He slashed me across the face with the gun barrel hard enough to knock me backwards over a chair. He was on me again before I could get up, kicking at my ribs with his steel-toed boots. I curled into a fetal ball and tried to roll away from the kicks. He dug his fists into the cloth of my shirt and dragged me toward him. I went with the pull and tried to twist around far enough to land a kick on his legs. It didn't work.

Finally my thrashing broke his hold on me. I rolled away and scrambled to my feet. I spat blood on the floor, breathing hard.

Hayes stood five feet away, his face knotted in rage, his breath coming in short, heavy rasps. His heavy muscular bulk made him look like a bear. He had the gun out again. The Army-issue .45 looked like a toy in his oversize hands. He raised the gun slowly, aiming at my heart. Then he dropped it on the floor and kicked it away.

"I'd rather," he said in a sharp harsh whisper, "kill you with my hands."

I aimed a spinning kick at his left knee and connected with my heavy hiking boot. The kick shattered his knee-cap. Most men would have fallen on the ground screaming in pain. Hayes took two steps forward.

I hit him twice in the face with solid jabs that caused him nothing more than mild irritation. As I brought a right cross around with my weight behind it he stepped inside the punch and hit me with a fist like a brick on the point of my cheekbone.

I could feel the bone break, nothing more, and then suddenly I fell into the pain like falling into a tank of water. The pain surrounded me. I swam in it.

Hayes picked me up off the floor like a child picking up a rag doll. He turned me in his grasp. An arm like an iron bar closed across my throat.

I got one hand underneath that bar before it closed and I pushed at the arm, fighting it off my throat. I clawed at it with my free arm until I had blood and flesh under my nails. I kicked back with my heels and stomped on his feet. It was like scratching at stone.

A dark red haze began to shroud my eyes. There was a roaring in my ears that I could not stop. The arm closed tighter. The world got smaller.

After a while I heard a voice. It was very faint and far off, like a voice you might hear calling your name when you are waking from sleep. This voice didn't call any names.

"Okay, fucker, put him down," it said.

The arm's vise grip on my throat loosened a quarter inch. A little air began to leak through my throat. I lunged for the air, trying to drink it down like a man lost at sea who has gone too long without fresh water. The red haze cleared a little. I saw Bernstein standing across the room. He was pointing Hayes's own automatic at him.

"Put him down now," he said, "or I'll kill you. You know I'll do it."

Hayes dragged me up from my knees, holding me in front of him as a shield. He laughed harshly. "You don't dare try it," he said scornfully. "I can snap this man's neck in a second. Besides," he added, with a sneer that bellied up from years of concealed hatred, "I never met a lousy Jewboy yet who could do the right thing when he had to."

Bernstein smiled, a slow, lazy, otherworldly smile. "Wrong," he said. Then he took two quick smooth steps forward, stuck the muzzle of his gun into Hayes's left eye, and blew the son of a bitch straight to hell.

CHAPTER 19

After the shot I lay on the floor of the office, breathing hard. The sound of the blast still rang in my ears. The left side of my face burned from the powder flash of the automatic.

Eventually the ringing subsided enough for me to hear what Bernstein was saying.

"You were in here too long," he said. "I had to leave Patty outside, in the warehouse. Are you going to be okay enough to take care of yourself while I go and get her?"

"I think so," I croaked, holding both hands to my throat. It was bruised, and the swelling was making it hard to talk. "Hayes had two people with him. Griggs and Keith Miller. Griggs went outside to check for cops. Miller's someplace in the warehouse. You'd better find Patty before he does."

"Okay." Bernstein helped me to my feet, took my gun from the desk top, and put it back in my hand. He let go and I swayed like a drunk in a strong wind. "Not so good," he said. "Better stay behind Hayes's desk, on the floor. Shoot anything coming in that isn't me."

"I'll try."

"Good." Bernstein helped me behind the desk. "By the way," he added maliciously, "how'd you like your little brush with mortality?"

"Didn't. It's painful, and there's no encore performance."

He laughed softly. He was about to turn and leave when we both heard the dragging of a foot on the concrete floor outside the office door. The door was open. Bernstein dropped into a crouch beside me.

There was a muffled cry. Patty and her brother burst into the office. Keith was holding her, one arm wrapped around her waist. With the other arm he held the wide sharp blade of a folding buck knife to her throat.

Keith saw Hayes's body lying on the floor, the wide square head leaking blood and tissue, the blackened crater where the eye had once been. His eyes opened wide with pain.

"What've you done!" he cried. He seemed to sag against Patty's back, but he didn't let her go. His short, heavy body shook all over. "The colonel, oh, God, you killed the colonel," he sobbed.

Bernstein spoke. "Let your sister go," he said, firmly but without anger. "You can't help anyone by killing her."

Keith slowly raised his head and opened his eyes, like a man coming out of shock. Grief mixed with rage and hate on his face. "You killed him, you kike," he hissed. "I'm going to kill you for that. But maybe I'll kill this bitch first."

He drew the wide knife blade slowly across Patty's neck. I watched with strangled horror. He didn't cut deeply, just enough through the skin to raise a red welt of blood along the cut.

Patty's eyes bulged out with fear and pain. But she closed her mouth and clenched her teeth to keep from crying out. When the cut was complete Miller pulled the knife away.

Patty spoke. "Keith, I'm sorry your friend was killed," she said softly. "I didn't mean to hurt you when I asked these men to look for you. I only did it because I was worried about you, and I wanted us to be together."

Keith again tightened the knife at her throat. "When have you ever cared about me?" he raged. "When? After Mom died you never came back to Colville Falls. You left me on my own. I hated you for it, but I learned to live with it. Now you come back, when I've got new friends, a new family, like, and you take them away too. You don't know about the colonel. He's done everything for me. He taught me how to shoot, how to fight, how to act. And he taught me the truth about the world. And you killed him. Oh God, I want to die." He shuddered, sobbing convulsively, an overgrown child.

Patty closed her eyes and began to weep silently. She ignored the dripping line of blood from the cut on her neck. When she opened her eyes again, she said, "Keith, please listen. I won't leave you alone again. If you come with me now we can help you. Matthew can make a deal with the government so that if you testify you won't have to go to jail for anything. Please, Keith. Please."

He straightened up again, still holding Patty tightly. For just a moment his eyes went blank, devoid of any emotion. "You don't understand," he said tonelessly. "It's too late. I killed that guy."

"Who?" I asked quickly. "Who did you kill, Keith?"

"No, Keith," Patty said quickly. "Don't say anything more."

"It doesn't matter," he replied in the same flat voice. "A man. I hit him. I killed—"

"Keith!" A sharp voice commanded from the door. Scott Griggs stood at an angle to the doorway, trying to

use the thin sheetrock walls as a shield. One of Bernstein's
.45 rounds would go right through the wall. Bernstein
began to crawl quietly away, looking for his shot.

"Shut up, kid. Just back out of the door slowly, and
we'll get the hell out of here."

Keith began to comply, dragging Patty with him as he
backed to the door. "What about the colonel?" he asked,
his voice agonized. "We can't just leave him here."

"That's what the colonel would tell us to do if he
could," Griggs replied gently. "You know what your duty
is. Do it."

Keith stopped when he reached the door. From behind
him Griggs called out, "Riordan? Listen to me. You and
the big guy just stay put in there. We're taking the girl
with us as far as the front door. If you don't come after us,
she'll be okay."

"No deal," I rasped in reply, tearing up my swollen
throat. "Leave her in the doorway, where we can see her.
Otherwise it's no deal. And you won't live long enough to
reach the street."

Griggs thought that one over. "Okay," he said finally.
"The woman steps back into the warehouse about three or
four feet. You can still see her. If she moves before we
leave, or if you come out of there, she's dead. Don't think
I won't shoot her in the back, because I will."

Bernstein snorted. "Honor among Aryans."

"Deal," I said quickly. Keith dragged Patty four or five
feet into the warhouse, outside the office door. She stood
alone, stiff and pale as a marble statue. We heard slow
footsteps as Griggs and Keith Miller backed away into the
gloom of the warehouse. Finally we heard running steps
that trailed away as they fled into the street.

Patty's iron self-control finally dissolved, eaten away by
the knowledge of her brother's crimes. She sagged down
until she sat cross-legged on the concrete floor of the

warehouse, elbows propped up on the top of her thighs. A thin line of blood ran like a red necklace around her throat. She buried her face in her hands and wept, inconsolable as a lost child.

Bernstein ran to the front door of the warehouse, then slowed before he reached the street. He walked back to where I sat on the floor beside Pats, my arms around her shaking shoulders. He had a look of savage satisfaction on his face.

"They're gone," he announced. "Fuck 'em. We've done enough, for now anyway. Now even the cops can find them." He laughed. "I wonder how well a couple of white-supremacy types are going to do at Walla Walla State Prison. I'll bet the local NAACP chapter will have a warm welcome for them."

I looked up at him and said nothing. Patty wept all the harder.

CHAPTER 20

By the time Miller and Griggs had fled, the long night had faded into cool gray morning. It was too late to try to sleep, so we tended to our wounds, physical and mental, at the emergency room of the local hospital. The on-duty sawbones was an officious young intern who insisted on being told exactly how Patty had received her throat wound before actually treating her. I tried assuring him in my best calm lawyer's voice that reports would be made to the proper authorities, so he should get on with it. When that didn't work, Bernstein less than calmly suggested that if the intern didn't get cracking he would find himself a patient. With severe internal injuries. That worked.

They bandaged Patty's cut and treated her for the light shock that was mixed equal parts of exhaustion and injury and fear for her brother. When her signs were near normal, the intern gave her a sedative and checked her into the hospital so that she could sleep. I wouldn't have minded a sedative myself, but all I got was an X-ray telling me that my cheekbone had been chipped, some stitching for the cut that Hayes's gun had left on my cheek, and one of those dumb-looking braces to take the strain off my bruised neck.

Bernstein and I found a hole-in-the-wall cafe near the hospital for breakfast, and Bernstein watched me try to swallow a little oatmeal and lukewarm tea, while he lingered over a double order of scrambled eggs and ham with home fries. He was amused.

"Just think, Riordan. This is what your old age is going to be like."

"At least you won't be around to be cute about it."

"Why?"

"Because somebody—possibly me—will shoot you by then."

He chuckled. "True. By the way, have you decided who we're going to tell about this mess? We have a body and a warehouse full of hazardous substances we're going to have to explain."

"As your lawyer, I've been giving those little technicalities some thought," I replied. "I think we should start with the Environmental Protection Agency. They've got a field office here. They're the ones who are going to have to deal with the wastes. And they're probably the only federal types around that don't move their lips when they read. So they might be some use in explaining all this to the county mounties."

"What about the FBI?"

"I'm sure they'll be invited to the party before it's over, but their nearest office is in Seattle. I want to stay local. We've got a better chance of staying out of jail if we go to the EPA and let them call in the local law. The county sheriff is going to be embarrassed enough finding a big-time crime operation right here in the apple country."

"Okay, I trust you. Get me a cell with a window."

"Come on," I growled, leaving the half-eaten oatmeal on the table. "Let's get it over with."

Wenatchee's small federal building was two blocks north of Main, on Sixth. It was built in the faceless GSA style popular in the 1960s, white concrete behind a small plaza, with blank-looking windows of black glass. We walked in through the double glass front doors and stood in the small, marblecrete-floored lobby, looking at a building directory. Before we found the right office, a passing secretary told us that the EPA was on the scond floor, in the back.

The EPA had just two small offices and a file room, hidden behind a beige metal door at the end of the building's back corridor. The first office was empty but for stacks of documents and a couple of IBM typewriters on the desks. The second office door was closed. I knocked.

"Come on in," a sandy, Texas-accented voice called out. I opened the door. A tall man, rail thin, was sitting with his big feet up on a metal desk. He had straight, dark blond hair, a long forehead, and a long straight nose. Beneath the nose a ragged Zapata mustache covered his mouth. He was somewhere between thirty-five and fifty, but his sun-weathered skin fit too well for me to guess.

"Good morning," the man said. "Name's Martin Ritt. What can I do for you?"

"We'd like to talk to the EPA's head bureaucrat," Bernstein said. Tact is not Bernstein's best thing.

"That's me," Ritt replied evenly. "I'm in charge here, in theory. But it's pretty hard to be a head bureaucrat when you're the only one in the office."

"You're the entire staff?" I asked, incredulously.

"Me and my secretary. Things have gotten a little thin since that old bastard took over," he said, gesturing at the government-issue portrait of Reagan that hangs in every federal office. Ritt's portrait was hanging upside down.

"You want lots of people, try the Department of Defense. They've got an airbase over at Spokane."

"We'd like to report a toxic waste dumping problem," I began hesitantly. "Really, an illegal dumping operation."

"Where are the dumps?" Ritt asked, not sure whether he should take me seriously.

"One of them is up in the Manzanita Valley, about ninety miles north of here. There's a gravel pit that's been used for dumping, and there's an old mine nearby, an abandoned gold or silver mine, that's got several dozen barrels of waste in it."

"Do you know what the chemicals involved are?"

"No."

"Then how do you know the waste is hazardous?"

"Because the barrels are leaking and the smell alone makes me gag."

"That's usually a pretty good sign, all right," Ritt drawled, a deadpan expression on his face. "Where's the second dump?"

"Uh, about four blocks from here."

"Four *blocks*!"

"Uh huh. A warehouse down on Columbia Street, near the railyards and the river."

Ritt shook his head, a skeptical look on his face. "And just how did you cowboys acquire this information?"

"We watched them dump the barrels, pal," Bernstein said heavily. "Then we followed them back down to Wenatchee, broke into their warehouse, and spotted more stuff. Okay? Now can we please get started and do whatever it is we have to do to get you idiots to take official notice of this little problem? Because I'd really like to get home, and frankly, man, you make my ass hurt just sitting there."

Martin Ritt remained at his desk, confused. "We've

never had a problem like this in the area. I'm going to have to call in an emergency team if you guys are on the level."

"We are," I assured him. "But there's one small complication."

"What's that?"

"There's a dead man in the warehouse. And another in the mine up in the Manzanita Valley."

Ritt sat back so hard that his head cracked the wall behind him. If it hurt, Ritt didn't notice it.

"Let me get this straight," he said slowly. "There are two dead men, one at each dump site. Why are they there? And who are they?"

"I'm not completely sure on the one body up in the mine. It may be the body of an environmental engineer named Larry Kramer."

"And the other?"

"Oh, I'm sure about him," Bernstein said. "His name was Hayes."

"Why are you sure?"

"I killed him."

Ritt gazed at us blankly, first at me, then at Bernstein. Slowly, he took in my damaged face, my swollen black eye, and the neck brace around my neck. Then he looked hard at Bernstein, noting the butt of the automatic sticking out from the shoulder holster under his half-open down vest, and the hard eyes that make grown men give him five feet of extra room as they pass him on the street.

Ritt finally spoke. "I think I'm beginning to believe you guys."

"Good. By the way," I added helpfully, "you should probably call the county sheriff's office, too, since there was a shooting involved."

"Uh. Right." He reached for the phone and began to dial.

Bernstein took out a cigarette and lit it, then looked around the room for an ashtray. Ritt looked up from his dialing and said, "I don't allow smoking . . . oh, hell, give me one of those. It's going to be one of those days."

Bernstein gave him a cigarette and sat back, a smile like a spoiled child's spread broadly across his face.

CHAPTER 21

We spent the rest of the day answering questions and preparing our statements for the EPA, the FBI, and the Chelan and Manzanita County sheriff's offices. The EPA had set up a temporary office in the conference room of the federal building. Three or four FBI agents and sheriff's deputies sprawled around the edges of the room, drinking coffee and smoking and whispering into telephones. We sat at a big wooden conference table in the center of the room. Before we were questioned I demanded, and got, the assistance of a federal public defender from Spokane in handling our statements. It delayed everything for two hours while he drove to Wenatchee, but it was worth it. I was exhausted and sore and jittery from the mixture of coffee and aspirin and codeine I was taking for the damage that Hayes had done to my face. The federal criminal code is no joke. It contains a number of crimes, like mail and wire fraud, that operate on the principle that its not what you've done, it's what it can be made to look like.

Patty was curled into a desk chair pulled up to the table. The FBI had brought her from the hospital. She bit her thumb and looked pensive. She said nothing. Nobody knew where her brother was.

We finished giving our statements a little after four o'clock. I watched idly as the court reporter carefully folded together the narrow, accordion-pleated pads of paper that had come out of her shorthand machine. She was flushed and sweaty from four straight hours of verbatim reporting. She was young and pretty, her hair cut in a loose style like Farah Fawcett used to wear. Styles last a long time in the country.

"I think that's everything," the FBI agent across the table said. His name was O'Keefe. He had thick black hair and bright pink skin. He kept his words clipped and professional, but he was clearly excited. This was the biggest thing he'd ever done.

The federal public defender's name was Lavelle. He said, "My clients are going to want to see the transcript before they sign their actual statements. How soon can we have a copy?"

O'Keefe looked at the reporter.

"Tomorrow, noon," she said. "If my computer is working right. Otherwise it will take a little longer."

"That's okay," O'Keefe replied. "Special Agent Broderick will be here tomorrow—"

"Just in time for the press conference," Bernstein drawled.

O'Keefe shot him a pained look. "Tomorrow, and he's probably going to want to talk to you three again. So please stay in the area tonight."

Lavelle knew his stuff. "You aren't planning charges, are you?" he asked quickly.

"That's not for me to say," O'Keefe replied. "But I don't see any." He packed his stuff into a scruffy plastic attaché case and followed the court reporter out of the room.

Lavelle stood up to go, a short stocky man with curling black hair and a beard that needed shaving three times a day. "I'm going to take off too," he said. He held out his hand and I shook it. "I'm staying at the Chieftain Motel, right in the middle of town, so call me if you've got any questions. We'll get together tomorrow. They aren't going to touch you, you know. You're going to be heroes."

Bernstein glared at him. "That's not," he growled, "what anybody here fucking had in mind."

"I know that," Lavelle replied evenly, "but you're stuck with it. So long." He left.

There was silence. Bernstein stood up and walked over behind Patty and began to massage her shoulders. She sagged a little under his strong touch. The skin-deep cut in her throat was bandaged and probably sore. But she almost smiled.

"I want you to know," he said, "that I'm sorry about your brother. I really am. Not for what he is. But for you."

She reached back and patted his hand. "Thank you. I used to wonder, when I was interviewing families of criminals—mothers, girlfriends, boyfriends—what it felt like. I wondered, but I didn't really care. Now I know."

"Matthew told me a little about your relationship with Keith," Bernstein said. "You think you're responsible for the way things have turned out with him. You're not."

"Who is?"

"He is."

She nodded.

Martin Ritt came back into the room and dropped into a chair across the table. He poured a cup of coffee from the carafe on the table, then reached across the table and took another of Bernstein's cigarettes.

"I quit six years ago," he said, lighting up, "and it's like I never stopped. Goddamn it."

"Have they found anything out?" I asked.

He looked at me bleakly. "A couple of things. The body in the mine was Larry Kramer's. As for the chemicals, the emergency team got here at noon. We've got a few people from our Seattle office, but most of them are from the Seattle Fire Department. They've got a real good chemical and atomic emergency squad. They started by analyzing the stuff in the warehouse that's still in barrels. It's a real witches' brew. We've got a lot of industrial solvents, benzene, carbon tetrachloride, trichlorethylene."

"Those are pretty common, aren't they?"

"Doesn't mean they're not toxic. Carbon tet may be toxic in levels below one part per million. But that's not the worst of it. We've also got pesticides and pesticide by-products like C-56. And I just got a report on the oil dumped up at the gravel pits. A lot of it may be just waste oil, from cars and such. But we're also picking up lots of PCBs, polychlorinated biphenyls. PCBs are often dissolved in oil. They're used that way, or were, in electrical trans- formers. PCBs are the worst. They aren't broken down by human or animal metabolisms. They concentrate in the fats and build up." He sighed. "We haven't tackled that mine yet. We're having additional environment suits and equip- ment shipped out. We'll need it."

"Has anybody contacted Montana Pacific yet?" I asked. "The gravel pit is on or near their property."

"Oh, yeah, we called them," Ritt replied. He gave me a crooked grin. "They got downright hostile when your name was mentioned, Riordan. But they've got some big problems. Much bigger than the gravel pit."

"What's that?"

"Ever hear of a town called Times Beach, Missouri?" Ritt asked. "It's a little town that used to be down on the Mississippi River there. A quiet place. Most of their streets were gravel or dirt, so they used to have a guy spray recycled oil on the roads to keep the dust down in the dry seasons. One summer the driver of the spray truck bought his oil from a recycler who was crooked as hell. The oil he got was transformer oil, full of PCBs. The town isn't there anymore. It was bought by the federal government. And it's being decontaminated, one street, one house, at a time."

"I don't follow."

"Montana Pacific has been taking gravel from those pits for its road construction and site work. If the gravel they used was laced with the contaminated oil, they aren't ever going to build a ski area. The only developing they're going to do is to put up a big fence with signs on it. The signs are going to say 'Warning. Contaminated Area.' "

The next day things got interesting. At one o'clock Randolph Whitten of Montana Pacific conducted a news conference at the construction site for the White Rose ski area. He arrived in a chauffeured jeep with leather seats and plush wool carpets. He wore corduroy slacks with a tweed jacket, just like a country gentleman. He had style. What he said had no more than a passing acquaintance with the truth.

He stood on a hastily built platform with a couple of microphones taped to the podium. The television mini-camera crews stood well back. Beneath the podium was a small crowd of eight or ten local and Seattle reporters. The four of us—Bernstein, Patty, Martin Ritt, and I—stood well off to one side. Several of the reporters in the group knew Patty. They stared at her with open curiosity.

"Our company had a dream," Whitten began sadly. "A dream of building a place where skiers and sportsmen could come to enjoy these beautiful mountains. A dream that would provide jobs for people in this valley who used to work in logging and mining, to replace those industries which, sadly, are probably lost forever. This dream came both from the inspiration of our executives, and our one hundred years of serving the people of the Pacific Northwest.

"Today, I must tell you frankly, our dream is on hold. Yesterday we learned that a gang of unscrupulous criminals had dumped terrible, toxic poisons on land owned by our company and others. Until we know the extent of the environmental damage which has been wrought to this beautiful land, we are suspending construction of the White Rose ski area. Montana Pacific is cooperating fully with state and federal law enforcement and environmental agencies to learn the extent of the damage that has been done. And to bring the bastards—I'm sorry, but that is what they are—the bastards who have done this to justice."

Whitten's words were still hanging in the thin mountain air when the little knot of reporters began hammering him with questions.

"Mr. Whitten, have any of the police groups identified the members of the gang that did this?"

"I'm sorry, you'll have to direct those questions to the FBI or to the Chelan and Manzanita County authorities. I understand that they will be making statements in Wenatchee this afternoon at three o'clock."

One of the Seattle reporters spoke up. "Mr. Whitten, is there any relationship between this problem and the death of Bernard Seaton, one of your company's attorneys?"

Whitten's face flushed deeply. "That is a cruel and irresponsible rumor," he said. His eyes scanned over the crowd. He found me and stared. I stared back. "If the source of this rumor can be traced, I'm sure that both our company and Mr. Seaton's family will be most willing to take legal action."

Whitten answered a few more questions the same way, with what politicians call the non-denial denial. It was perfected during Watergate. You never answer the question. Instead, you call the question stupid or scandalous or shocking, and go on to the next question.

A few minutes later a short round company flack in an ill-fitting gray suit stepped to the podium. He didn't like these questions at all. "Thank you, ladies and gentlemen," he cut in, "but Mr. Whitten has much work to do to assist the authorities. If you have any other questions they can be referred to our offices in Seattle."

The press conference broke up. I turned to Martin Ritt. "He was kind of long on prose and short on information," I said.

"That's normal," he shrugged. "They've got a big public black eye and a big bill to pay. Under the law, they may be financially responsible for cleaning up their property, even if the dumping was not their fault."

"They can afford it," I said. "Better than many others."

"True."

I saw Whitten striding to the edge of the meadow where his jeep was parked. I broke away from my group and walked over to cut him off. When he saw me he swerved and kept on walking. I had to step in front of him again to stop him.

He stood in front of me. His mouth was closed, jaw muscles working, his gray eyes flashing with anger. Eventually he spoke.

"Riordan," he said with icy control. "Haven't you done enough?"

"I did exactly what I was paid to do, Mr. Whitten. I found Larry Kramer. His body is in the mine above the gravel pit. The police will tell you that shortly, if they haven't already."

"Then get out of my way," he grunted.

"I wanted to tell you one other thing," I said. "When the killer of Bernie Seaton is identified, then I'll be through. And only then."

"Get out." He stepped around me and strode to his car. I walked back to where the others were standing.

"Am I missing something here?" Martin Ritt said.

"Not really," I told him. "We going back to town?"

"I need to stop up at the waste site," he answered. "Do you mind riding along? It won't take very long."

"Let's go."

Martin Ritt drove us up to the gravel pit on the old logging road connecting it to the ski area. He stopped at the trailer that the EPA had set up for workers at the site.

"I won't be long," he said as he went into the trailer.

Bernstein and Patty and I walked over to the pit itself. The EPA site teams had secured the gravel pit, mounting a temporary wire fence laced with barbed wire and dotted with red warning signs. Inside the compound, the removal crews worked in white environment suits, the twin snouts of their rebreathers making them look like the aliens in a 1940s horror magazine. Slowly, carefully, they removed the PCB and dioxin-laced gravel and placed it into drums. The drums would be taken to Pasco, Washington, down on the Columbia River, to wait out the months or years until a safe, reliable high-temperature incinerator could be built. The people who lived in the valley would have to wait as well. In ten years, fifteen years, they would know whether or not the dumping had been stopped soon enough to keep it from poisoning the water supply. They would watch for cancers, for sores that didn't heal, and eventually they would know.

Martin Ritt walked over to join us. He scuffed the heel of his boot into the dirt as he watched the wastes being removed. He turned to me and said, "We've gotten no place on trying to track where the wastes came from. It looks to me like it was brokered to Hayes and his bunch through some kind of middleman. We searched the warehouse, and the FBI have searched Hayes's home and office. Hayes had no records at all." He frowned, then added, "We scheduled our inspections kind of early this morning at some of the Northwest and California companies that would produce these kinds of wastes in their businesses. They just smiled and showed us their transport manifests and invited us to look around. We can't prove a thing. The waste could have come from anywhere. Anywhere at all."

As we walked back to Ritt's old Bronco, an FBI agent at the site who was cataloging the gravel samples as evidence came striding over to us. "Are you Patricia Miller?" he asked Patty.

"Yes, I am. What is it?" Her breath caught like fear in her throat."

"You asked to be notified if your brother was located."

"Where is he?"

"We don't know exactly. But he robbed a bank in Centralia about two hours ago."

CHAPTER 22

They caught up with Keith Miller two days later, holed up in a battered turn-of-the-century farmhouse by the shore of the Chehalis River, not forty miles from the bank he had robbed in Centralia, Washington. The house supposedly belonged to a man named Dorsey Butler, an elderly farmer and coal miner with a taste for the guns-and-hellfire preaching of Robert Birdsall. The FBI was waiting outside his house now, with real guns and real fire, and I wondered if the old man still liked the taste.

Patty and I drove down from Seattle as fast as we dared. She worried about Keith out loud for the first fifty miles or so, then lapsed into pensive silence. As I turned off the interstate into Cowlitz County, she sat silently, watching the gray sky and low, dark fir-covered hills as dusk approached. By the time we reached the Chehalis River, the moon had risen, and its light danced on the mist rising from the river marshes.

The farmhouse was two stories tall, a plain honest house with high windows and a wide porch that had fallen on evil times. The paint was peeling, the eaves were rotted, and the roof was covered with moss. The porch was broken down, sagging like a man on crutches. It was a house where dreams ended.

The FBI had circled the house and the surrounding farm buildings. Two heavy-duty weapons trucks had been parked in the front pasture, nearest the road. Quartz-beam floodlamps, powered by a whining diesel generator, bathed the farmhouse in harsh white light. A battle line flanking the trucks had been set up, running past the house to the barns and chicken coop. To the rear of the house, on the river side, flares had been laid down, glowing hot yellow like a grass fire. In the reeds at the river's edge I knew snipers would be waiting.

The young FBI agent controlling traffic on the road running by the farmhouse led us through the crowd of FBI agents, press, and sheriff's deputies when Patty explained that her brother was one of the men holding the house. He took us to the command-center truck at the edge of the pasture in front of the house. A short man with a pudgy, desk-bound body stood at the back of the truck facing into it through its open back doors. He was wearing tight-fitting khaki fatigues, a bulletproof kevlar vest, and a black unmarked baseball-type cap. A fat man playing soldier.

"Tell the men down by the river to stay under cover," he said into a radio headset. "If they try to come out that way, I want our people to shoot at the first hostile move. They don't have to wait for gunfire."

He put the headset down and turned around.

"I'm Special Agent Broderick, in charge of this operation. You must be Patricia Miller." When he saw me he sighed and added, "And you, Riordan, what the fuck are you doing here?"

"I represent Ms. Miller, Broderick. She's come down here to help you, to try to talk her brother and the other man out of that house."

Broderick gave me a cold impatient look and turned back to Patty.

"I appreciate your wanting to help, Ms. Miller," he said, "but I'm afraid there isn't much I can do for you here."

"How long have the negotiations been going on?" Patty asked.

"We aren't attempting to negotiate, miss."

"What do you mean you're not trying to negotiate," I cut in harshly. "You are not fucking G.I. Joe, Broderick. This is not a war. You do not have the right to use force as a first resort."

"Don't you tell me my job, Riordan," he said fiercely, stabbing a finger into my chest. "This is not a hostage situation. Both of the scumbags in that house are fanatics. Last year we had two agents shot and wounded by members of The Order, a group related to the one that Miller belongs to. I'm not risking any of my agents' lives here."

"Please," Patty said desperately. "Please stop it, both of you. Give me a chance to talk to my brother. That's all I'm asking for."

I shut up. Broderick fumed silently, a petty bureaucrat fearful of giving in on anything, no matter how small, lest some other petty bureaucrat label him weak. "All right," he said finally. "We've tied into the telephone in the house. Whenever you're ready, just pick up the red handset in the comm truck." He walked away to confer with his men.

Patty stood stock-still for a moment, eyes closed, gathering up her wits to talk to her brother. I paced anxiously around the back of the truck with small slow steps, unable to decide if I should stick close or step away while Patty tried to persuade her brother to keep on living.

She stepped to the back of the truck and reached inside

for the telephone. She picked it up slowly. "It's ringing," she said softly.

She waited. "Keith?" she said finally. "Keith, honey, it's Patty." She listened. She shook her head.

"Keith, I'm here because I want to help you," she insisted. "What's happened between us over the years can't be forgotten, but it can be changed."

She listened again, then shook her head. "Keith, please," she begged. "I can get you a good lawyer. You'll have to go to prison if you're guilty, but it won't be forever. You'll still have a life." She was silent again.

Patty listened for what seemed like a long time. Her body began to shake, and she wept, painfully. "Keith, no," she whispered. "Please tell me that's not . . . wait. Wait." She clenched the phone tightly in her hand. I stepped to her and put my arms around here. She still held the phone. I could hear the dial tone. "He's gone," she whispered.

Broderick returned. He looked at me with the question in his eyes. I shook my head.

Broderick reached into the truck and pulled out a bull-horn. He stepped to the edge of the pasture in front of the house, clearly visible in the harsh white light. The television crews behind us switched on their cameras as they fought for a clear view of the house.

"This is the FBI," he said. "You have one minute to surrender. Then we will take the house." For a reply he got the flat crack of a hunting rifle from inside the house. The shot dropped Broderick flat on his face in the muddy front pasture. He got up sputtering, spitting mud. Keith Miller had a very nasty sense of humor.

There was a rattle of return fire from the FBI forces and sheriff's deputies ringing the house. Broderick cut off the fire with a hand gesture. "One minute," he repeated. He wiped some mud off his face.

The front door slammed open and a white-haired man with a wisp of white beard stepped out on the front porch. He stood in silhouette, his gaunt hawklike features picked out in sharp relief. "Don't hurt me," he shouted in a querulous, high-pitched voice. "I'm surrendering." He ran in a low crouch across the pasture, stumbling into the arms of two agents. They knocked him to the ground and searched him as he lay face first in the mud, then cuffed him and led him away.

Broderick took out his bullhorn again. "Mr. Miller," he said, "you have no hope. Come out now."

There was no answer.

Broderick stepped back to the comm truck and took out a headset and put it on. "Get ready," he said, speaking softly into the small mike.

"Broderick, wait," I pleaded. "The kid is twenty-two years old. He's alone, he's scared. You can cut off his water, his electric, starve him out or freeze him out. Use tear gas if you have to. Inside of twenty-four hours you'd have him."

"So what?" he said savagely. "That isn't some nice boy in there, Riordan. He had his shot to take me out and he missed. Now I get mine."

"He wasn't aiming at you, Broderick. You know that. He just wanted to knock you down a little. When you get this kid you'll be able to break him easily. He could tell you a lot."

"I haven't got time for that, Riordan. The longer he's in there, the more chance there is for him to get lucky and hit one of my people. I won't take that chance." He turned back toward the house and spoke into the microphone of his headset. "George, let's illuminate the scene."

There was a muffled *crump* behind me as a phosphorus flare grenade was launched. It crashed through the front picture window of the house, filling it with burning white light.

Keith Miller opened up with an automatic rifle on the FBI troops from a kitchen window at the front left corner of the house. I knew he couldn't see very well because of the glaring lights from the trucks. Most of the rounds he fired plowed into the muddy front pasture.

Broderick spoke into the headset again. "Return fire. Keep the bastard pinned down. George, try to get a flare into the room he's in."

The second flare hit too high on the wall and fell to the ground outside, igniting the weathered wooden siding of the house. The third flare broke through the kitchen window and burst into life. The room began to burn. There was an anguished throaty scream, a scream I remembered from the war. A scream that burning men scream.

Keith was still screaming when an old kerosene-fired water heater in the kitchen exploded into a roiling ball of oily flame. The explosion swelled brightly against the black sky. Then it faded, and the only sound we heard was the steady roar of the fire.

I looked at Broderick. He was trying to keep his face blank, but there was a light of triumph in his eyes and a faint smile on his lips as he pulled them back, baring his teeth.

I said nothing. I just stood and waited and held Patty tightly in my arms.

CHAPTER 23

Two weeks to the day after the FBI killed Keith Miller, I was back at work in the King County Courthouse. During those two weeks I thought a great deal. I thought some about Keith Miller as I tried to help Patty work through her grief, but Keith seemed no more or less than what he was, a confused boy in love with a stronger, older man who had shown him a way of living that seemed cold and hard and clear. I thought some about Wilbur Hayes, but I understood the nature of his corruption no more than I had in the moment when he nearly choked the life from me. Bernstein said I should reread Conrad. I said I would settle for Hayes being dead.

Mostly I thought about Bernie Seaton.

I spent my first morning back at work waiting for a little two-day auto accident case to be called for trial. At the morning calendar call the clerk said that no courtroom would be available for at least another week, so I stepped out of the presiding judge's courtroom to call my client. On my way to the phone I ran into Vincent Ahlberg.

He was standing in one of the bleak gray marble corridors, smoking one of his little cigars, chatting amiably with an old lawyer I didn't know. The old man was tall, spare, and elegant, with a great head of wavy white hair and a strong wide chin and jaw that dominated his face. But the old man's nose was a reddish mass of broken blood vessels, and his eyes were rheumy and yellow. Bourbon fumes wafted in the air. It was not quite eleven o'clock in the morning. The old man mumbled a polite greeting and shuffled away.

"That was Halsey Roberts," Vince said in lieu of a greeting. "He used to be damned good." He shook his head.

"Occupational hazard," I said, more glibly than I felt. "What brings you down here?"

"Testifying in the Lorenz murder. Should have known they'd be running late; the defendant has got Willets defending him, and Willets will make love to a jury for hours before letting things get started. Anyway," he added, "how's your friend Patricia holding up?"

"Okay, I think. She buried her brother at home, in Colville Falls. She's back at her desk at the newspaper now." I hesitated. "I think I know what you want to ask, Vince. The answer is that for a while I thought it was going to work this time. That she would stay. But I don't think so any more."

"I'm sorry," Vince said.

"Me too. So," I said, changing the subject, "have you heard anything from the FBI on Griggs?"

"They still haven't found him, if that's what you mean. He's gone to ground pretty thoroughly. I wish we could get him. Until we do, I can't close the file on Bernie Seaton. I've got to believe that either he or Miller killed Seaton because of that mess you uncovered over in the Manzanita Valley."

"I'm pretty sure I agree with you," I said slowly. "But

there's a couple of things that bother me. Small things, but the farther I get away from the case, the more they stand out.''

"Like what?''

"The timing of Bernie's killing. Bernie didn't know anything about the problems at the White Rose area when he died. When I was hired, Kramer was already dead. Kramer hadn't said anything to Bernie before he died; Bernie was as much in the dark as anybody else. I had just started working the day before Bernie was killed, and I didn't find anything out, except following that lead about Kramer over to Idaho. I told Bernie about that over the phone, just a couple hours before he was killed. Neither of us thought it meant much at the time. So why was he killed at that particular time?''

Ahlberg shrugged. "The same reason Miller tried to take you out on the highway, I suppose. To prevent you from finding out what happened to Kramer, and tracing that back to the chemical dumping. And to scare off Montana Pacific from developing that ski area.''

"Maybe,'' I said doubtfully. "But that raises another problem. Bernie was killed around two-thirty in the morning. It's over five hours' road time from Seattle to Darien. Miller and Griggs couldn't have gotten to Darien until eight o'clock in the morning, at the earliest. They went after me at about ten-thirty or eleven, on the highway, nearly fifty miles south of Darien. That's good. That's too good.''

"It's possible.''

"Yeah, but to get to Darien, find me, figure out who I am and what I'm doing, get on my tail, hold the tail for fifty miles without being spotted, all within a couple of hours? That's pushing reality. Unless . . .''

"Unless somebody in the company told them who you

were and what to look for," Vince said. "Hey!" he added
as I started to back away, "where in hell are you going?"

"I'm going to check out a couple of things," I told him.
"I'll call you tonight."

He started to follow. The door to the courtroom opened
behind him and a bailiff waived him in. "Shit," he hissed.
He walked into the courtroom, turning once to glare at me.

When I got back to my office I settled down with a pot
of strong black French-roast coffee and a large sketch pad
that I use for outlining the facts I plan to present to the jury
in a trial. I laid out on the pad everything I knew about the
chemical dumping at the White Rose development, Miller's involvement with Hayes, and Seaton's death.

At first the facts were clear. The EPA technical people
had estimated that the dumping at the White Rose site had
been going on for a year or more. Kramer had moved to
the White Rose site a long time after the dumping had
started. The only logical conclusion was one that the FBI
and the EPA had already drawn: Kramer had discovered
the dumping, had been bought off, and then changed his
mind. That got him killed.

Someone at Montana Pacific must have known of the
dumping from the beginning when Kramer found out about
it. That person had been the contact point for Hayes to buy
off Kramer.

It wasn't Bernie. That was a judgment on my part, but I
knew it was right. Bernie would have regarded an offer of
a bribe the same way he would an offer to sell him a slave.
The thought of accepting just would not occur to him.
Horatio Alger. Dick Diver. To the end.

I had to assume someone else. Bernie hired me to find
Kramer. I found out only one thing: that Kramer needed
money because he was in the depths of some kind of male
menopause, drinking, gambling, in love with a whore. I
called Bernie and gave him that fact. Was that enough to

kill him? No. Killing him was a huge risk. It had to be something else.

The only way that Miller and Griggs could know that I was in Darien the morning after Bernie died was for someone at the Montana Pacific office to tell them. They had to be told the same morning I left for Seattle. There was only one person in the Darien office the two times I was there.

Fedders. Doug Fedders.

What else was Bernie working on that night? Think. He was tracing land titles, mineral rights claims. Claims for what. Gravel. Who was designing the roads being built before construction would start on the ski area? Roads need gravel.

Doug Fedders.

I wrote his name in capital letters and underlined it twice.

Fedders might still be at the Montana Pacific offices in Darien. I took out my beat-up leather address book, found the number, reached for the phone, and dialed.

He answered on the second ring. "Montana Pacific Darien office," he said.

"Doug Fedders? This is Matthew Riordan in Seattle."

"Mr. Riordan," he said hesitantly. "I'm not supposed to be talking to you."

"Who says?"

"Mr. Whitten. I think he blames this, uh, mess on you."

"I heard the project was shut down. I'm sorry."

"So am I," he said sadly. "I'm just stunned by the whole thing, the chemical dumping going on right under our noses. And the suspicion that Larry was involved makes it worse. I feel used, man. Degraded. Anyway," he sighed, "we're keeping the office open for a couple more weeks to assist the EPA, but that's it. I've been laid off, as of next month. So what do you need? I guess I can talk to you, they can't do anything else to me."

"You're right. And it's important. The Seattle police are still not sure who killed Bernie Seaton. I just thought of something that might help them, but I need some information from you. Can you find the legal description of the gravel pit land where the dumping took place?"

"Sure, I think so. We have a file on each area we planned to take road or building material from. I've had them all out in the past couple of days. The EPA wants to check all the land in the area."

I heard a heavy *thunk* as he set the phone down on his desk top. He returned a minute later. "Riordan? Here it is." He read off the legal description by the geologic survey system that we use in the West—section, township, and range. "That's it. Ashworthy Timber is the surface owner. Anything else?"

"What else is in that file?"

"Some estimates of the volume of gravel we could take. And here's a note. Shit. It's in Larry's handwriting."

"What does it say?"

"It says, 'No reservation of minerals—will Seaton find out? Must know if we're covered.' That's it. Does it mean something?"

"Listen to me carefully, Fedders. There's a couple of lawyers in Darien. I want you to take that note over to a lawyer's office, right in the file where you found it. Give the whole file to the lawyer. Make a statement in writing, in his office, about how you found it. Sign it and have it witnessed. Do it now."

"I don't know" he said hesitantly. "The company—"

"The company my ass," I said hotly. "How much did they pay you, Fedders? Whatever it was, it wasn't enough, because I am personally going to have your butt kicked into jail for about a hundred years."

"I don't know what you're talking about," he said, breathing heavily. His voice was half angry, half scared. "I didn't know about this. Any of it. Not the dumping, not the"—he hesitated— "murders. Nothing. I swear."

"That's not good enough," I said harshly. "You've got half an hour to get to a lawyer, give him that evidence, and have him call me. And don't even think about running. If I don't get that call, I'm going to do two things. First, I'm going to call the cops. Second, I'm going to call a friend of mine. He's in the removal business. Both of them will be looking for you, Fedders. It'll be a race. To see who finds you first." I let the threat hang in the telephone static. Then I hung up.

The minutes walked by on tiptoe, slowly, quietly. I paced around my office, straightening loose papers, scratching out notes. I got up and opened a beer and stepped out on my deck. I couldn't drink the beer. I walked back in and sat down. I remember waiting being easier when I used to smoke.

The phone rang twenty-two minutes later. I felt buzzy, short of breath. I picked it up.

"Mr. Riordan?" a quiet, gently grave voice asked. "My name is Grayson, sir. William Grayson. I am an attorney in Darien, in Manzanita County." He hesitated.

"Yes, counsel?" I replied.

"I have a Mr. Fedders in my office. He seems quite upset. He wishes to make a statement and entrust some evidence into my care."

"That's correct, Mr. Grayson. Please take his statement and witness it. Fedders is holding important evidence in a murder investigation. I suggest you make photocopies of everything, and place the evidence in a bank safe, preferably not at your usual bank. And please, sir, for your own safety, do not discuss this matter with anyone."

"I am always discreet, Mr. Riordan," he said gravely.

"I will do as you ask." A hint of a chuckle crept into the man's solemn voice. "Thank you. I am eighty-one years old, sir. I haven't had this much excitement in years."

"Thank you. Please send me a bill."

"I will. Do you have anything to tell Mr. Fedders?"

"Yeah. Tell him to relax."

The hint of a chuckle came back into his voice. "I think he will be very happy to hear that, sir. Good day." The old man rang off.

I sat back in my chair, feeling a rush of excitement and relief. I knew who killed Bernie Seaton. I even thought I could prove it, with a couple of yards of luck. I had one or two more things to check. I got busy.

CHAPTER 24

I got to the Montana Pacific Building a little before six that evening. The building was quiet, clearing out but not yet empty. Even on the West Coast, where people think that working New York hours is a sign of advanced mental illness, being upwardly mobile means not being the first person the boss sees going out the door.

I took the elevator to the executive floor and walked silently toward Randolph Whitten's office, my footsteps swallowed by the thick carpeting. As I passed open office doors, the residents looked up but ignored me. I was just another guy in a pinstriped suit of corporate gray. They didn't see the Walther automatic in the Burns & Martin snap-down holster.

Whitten's office was at the end of the hall, two doors down from the company chairman's. His secretary was missing from her desk. I opened both of the double walnut doors to his office and stepped through.

Whitten was sitting on the edge of his marble conference table, jacket off, tie loosened. An elegant brunette in a creamy white cashmere sweater-dress sat in a chair to his side. She was laughing. Whitten was smiling. The boss had just told a joke.

She stood up, startled by my entrance. Her long dark hair flowed to her shoulders. Her face was pretty but confused.

"You can't come in here, sir," she said firmly.

"Sure I can. I just did."

"But sir . . ." she broke off and looked at Whitten. He was looking at me, a sneer on his long aristocratic face. She started for the telephone. Whitten raised a hand.

"It's all right, Carol," he said heavily. "Go on home. I can take care of this"—he gestured with his eyes toward me— "little problem. I'll see you in the morning."

Whitten and I watched silently as she walked to her desk outside and got her coat and purse. Still puzzled, she glanced back at us one more time as she walked down the hallway to the elevators. Whitten got up and closed the doors, then leaned against them, facing me.

"We've really got you by the balls, you know," he said conversationally. "I've been talking with my lawyers. They're still trying to decide whether to sue you or just put the word on the street about how you bungled the work we asked you to do. I lean toward putting the word out, myself. I think it'll be fun to watch you dry up and blow away."

"Don't be silly," I said mildly. "You're not going to have time to do any of that. You'll be too busy defending a murder charge."

He laughed disdainfully. "You're getting ridiculous, Riordan. Really paranoid. You're a small little man who's blown the big one. This fantasy isn't going to help you." Whitten strolled back to the conference table and sat down. "Okay. Who did I kill?"

"Bernie Seaton," I replied. "At two-thirty in the morning, in the parking garage. With a tire iron."

"This is crazy," he said. "I'm leaving." He stood up from the table. He took a step toward the door.

I hit him just once, a right cross that came from the shoulder with maybe a little more punctuation than I intended. It sprawled him back across his expensive executive table like a sack of loose laundry. He sat up slowly, legs dangling over the edge of the table, blood leaking from his mouth. He dabbed at the blood with a handkerchief.

"You went into business with Wilbur Hayes over a year ago," I began. "Maybe longer. Don't tell me you didn't know Hayes, you did. You show up a half-dozen times on the donor list of the American Freedom Foundation, going back three years. There's a photograph of the two of you in the *Post*'s newspaper morgue at a campaign dinner for Guy Akers, that right-wing mayor from Pasco who ran for the Senate last year."

He shrugged. "So I knew Wilbur Hayes slightly. So what?" The fat lip I had given him made him mumble.

"That's an interesting little fact you left out of your statement to the FBI on the Manzanita waste dump," I said. "But there's more. Lots more.

"You went into the dumping business with Hayes. Maybe some of the toxic waste came from your own company at first, I don't know. You selected the Manzanita site because it was one of the most remote pieces of real estate the MP owned that was still close enough to make dumping there cheap."

"You can't—"

"Shut up. Or I'll shut you up. Seven months ago the chairman of your company had the brilliant idea for a ski resort, a place he could take his grandchildren and say, 'Wasn't Grandpa a big guy? He built this.' The chairman started out as a surveyor for the railroad, years ago. He knows the land the MP holds. He knew just the place. Jack Pine Mountain, right at the head of the Manzanita Valley.

But Jack Pine doesn't sound good enough, so your flacks went to work and came up with the new name. White Rose.'' I stopped and looked at him. He no longer looked bored. He looked ill. But his eyes were alive and full of purpose. He was thinking. I went on.

"By then the dumping had started. Bernie said you tried hard to kill the project, or move it. But the chairman wouldn't budge. So the survey team was set up in Darien. Eventually Kramer discovered that the water draining from the area was polluted. You paid him off, set him to work trying to screw up the project.

"Eventually, Kramer changed his mind and came to you. That was a mistake. You knew that he'd needed the money you were paying him, and why. You set him up with Hayes. And Hayes or his troops killed him."

Whitten said nothing. He simply stood up and walked to his desk. He sat down behind it and reached for his telephone, pausing with one hand on the receiver.

"Are you going to stop this, Riordan? Or do I call the cops and have them haul you away?"

"Call away," I said. "Let's both go tell our stories."

He took his hand from the phone and dropped it in his lap.

I took out my Walther and pointed it at him. "Hands on the desk top, where I can see them," I said.

He complied.

"Going on. When Kramer was killed, you thought you had the problem licked. The project would be tied up in lawsuits and set back until it was dropped. Then Bernie insisted on hiring me. And the chairman and Bernie's boss, the general counsel, backed Bernie up.

"You found out, from Kramer, that there was a problem with the gravel pits you were using. The Montana Pacific simply didn't own the mineral rights on that land. When the surface owners sued because of the project and recovered their rights, there might be testing to see how much mineral you'd taken without paying, to build roads. That might expose the dumps. On the night Bernie died, he was doing research to see if the landowners' claims were any good. When I talked to him on the telephone he knew that they were good claims. There were two people he told of that fact. Me. And you."

Whitten lowered his head. "We can work this out," he said huskily. He looked up. "There's money in this, Riordan, lots of money. More than I ever thought. I started this to solve our own problems. But Hayes found a lot of other businesses willing to pay a fortune to have the stuff taken off their hands."

"I'm not done," I told him. "When Bernie left the office that night you were waiting for him. I did some checking. You live alone, having safely exiled the wife and kids out to the suburbs. You've got a fancy condo in the Pike Place Market area, suitable for shacking up with stewardesses and other mid-life crisis sports. Nobody is going to be able to alibi you for that night, are they? But you thought you had it covered. The only person Bernie talked to that night was me. And you weren't worried about me tracing the mineral rights problem back to you, since I was going to buy it on the highway that same morning."

"I didn't kill Seaton," he said brokenly. "Miller did. Or Griggs. It was one of them. They used a tire iron, just like with Kramer."

"No, we didn't," a voice behind me said in a sandy southwestern drawl. "We were over in Darien, trying to pick up on old Riordan there."

I turned around very slowly and carefully, holding the Walther in the air. Scott Griggs stood behind me, his back to the closed office doors. There was a .45 service automatic in his hand. I hadn't heard a thing.

I dropped the Walther on the rug and kicked it toward Griggs. It hung up on the carpet and stopped halfway between us.

"Get his gun, Griggs," Whitten said. "I've got him covered." I half turned. Whitten held a small short-barreled revolver. Griggs inched forward carefully and picked up my piece.

"You guess pretty good, Riordan," Griggs said. "You always did. But the show is over."

"Not quite. Whitten here hasn't finished selling you down the river yet. He's going to, you know. Stick around and watch."

"I was just buying time, Griggs," Whitten said. "I knew you were coming."

"Sure you were. But time is what I haven't got. I want more money, Whitten, and I want out of the country. There's a night flight from Portland to LA. From there I can get to Mexico. I want to be on it tonight, and you're going to drive me to Portland to catch it."

"Absolutely, Scott. No problem. But first we've got to get rid of Riordan."

"How much money have you got for me?"

"Fifty thousand. Cash. Ready to go."

Griggs laughed harshly. "You bastard. You and Hayes cleared better than a million, that I know about. I've done prison time before. I'm tempted to put you in and go away for a while myself rather than have a smart-ass like you fuck me over."

"I'll get you more money."

"No, he won't," I cut in. "Griggs, you're not stupid. If he puts you on a plane there will be cops waiting at the other end for you. He's tried to sell you out to me, and I didn't have anything but guesswork. He'll kill you or turn you in." I started to back slowly away.

"Damn it, Griggs, take him out of here and kill him. Now."

"Okay." Griggs turned slowly toward me. But his feet did not move. They were still firmly planted, facing toward Whitten.

Whitten saw it too. He fired.

The shots didn't sound like much, two rapid little pops that straightened Griggs up and snapped his head back, as if in surprise. Griggs's .45 roared and blew a crater in the wall over Whitten's head. Griggs stumbled backward and fell with one round dark hole in his throat and another on the cheekbone, just beneath his left eye.

Whitten turned his gun on me. I stared back at him. His mouth was open, his features slack. His eyes were tortured, dull. He said nothing. There was a pounding on the office door.

I moved to open the door.

He spoke. "Stay back. I still have the gun."

"If you kill me, you'll have to kill them as well," I said, gesturing at the door. "And everyone who sees you in this building, or on the street. There aren't enough bullets in that gun, man. There aren't enough bullets in the world."

I walked to the doors and opened them. Two of the gray-suited junior executives I had seen down the hallway stumbled into the room, nearly falling over Griggs's body. They stared at the body and at the spray of blood and tissue on the wall behind it. One of them blanched and ran from the room, his hands clamped over his mouth.

To the other I said, "Mr. Whitten shot this man. Please call the police."

He stared at the black revolver wavering in Whitten's hand.

"Don't worry," I said gently. "Go."

He nodded quickly and left.

I turned back to Whitten. His features were still, almost lifeless, as though he'd suffered a stroke. "I really would have had a hell of a time proving a case against you," I said coldly. "But now I don't have to. You're all through. You know that. You've got a corpse on your floor that you can't possibly explain. And no corporate backup plan or press release or fall guy can make it go away."

Whitten nodded. He put the gun in his mouth. I turned my head away just as he fired.

CHAPTER 25

I walked silently past the loose knot of office workers gathered in the hallway outside Randolph Whitten's office. They let me pass without a word. But they looked at me strangely, with the wary eyes that civilians have for cops or soldiers. Or, as Bernie surely would have pointed out, the way we look at the insane.

I walked to the elevator and took it down one floor, to Bernie's old office. I don't know why I wanted to go there. Maybe I was tying to tell him, somehow, that I had done my job, that I had found Kramer, and found his killer. A foolish thought. Bernie was dead and could never know, or care. When you study law you learn that justice is solely for the benefit of the survivors.

Bernie's office had been filled. Standing behind his desk was a young lawyer of twenty-seven or twenty-eight. He was a handsome guy. He had blond hair and high cheekbones in an even-featured face. He wore a nicely tailored Italian-cut suit over a nicely maintained broad-shouldered body. He was unpacking and shelving a set of legal hornbooks that looked like they had never been opened. As a

lawyer he was probably about as useful as masturbation.
Maybe he would learn.

When he saw me standing in his office he was startled.
But he had his natural arrogance back in place by the time
he spoke.

"Who the hell are you?" he said.

"My name is Riordan. What are you doing in here?"

"What do you mean, what am I doing? This is my
fucking office. What's the matter with you?" He pointed
to a nameplate on his desk. It said his name was Geoffrey
Craven. With a "G." Figured.

"Nothing," I replied. "This used to be Bernie Seaton's
office."

"Who? Oh, the guy that got killed. Now what do you
want? I've got work to do."

"I want to see Bernie's things. Have you sent them to
his family?"

"I don't know."

"What do you mean, you don't know?" I walked
toward Craven steadily, with a slow measured step. I let him
see the anger building up in my eyes.

He backed away, a little shaken. "Look," he said
placatingly, his hands pushing the air in front of him, "I
think my secretary may have tried to figure out where to
send the stuff. Hell, what difference does it make?"

"It matters," I said as he backed into the corner of his
office. Then I saw that a cardboard box of thrown-together
stuff had been left near Bernie's bookcases.

I walked over to them, dropped to my knees, and sifted
through the box. Most of it was junk—a broken cigarette
lighter, plastic pens and rulers, a coffee cup from the last
United Way fund drive. The meaningless debris of one-
third of Bernie's life.

In the bottom of the box I found what I wanted—the
glass-covered picture frame containing Bernie's Vietnam

Silver Star and other medals. The frame had been carelessly tossed into the box. The glass had broken. No matter. It could be fixed.

I took the frame from the cardboard box and gently removed the broken glass. The medals looked fine. They belonged to a small boy. Maybe he would let me explain them to him someday.

I stood up to go. Craven was still backed up in the corner of his office, staring at me.

"These things matter," I told him. "In ways you could not possibly understand." I held the picture frame containing Bernie's medals carefully, in both hands, as I walked away.

About the Author

Fredrick Huebner is also the author of THE JOSHUA
SEQUENCE. An attorney, he lives in Seattle, Washington.